RED
MIDNIGHT

RED
MIDNIGHT

BEN
MIKAELSEN

 HarperCollinsPublishers

Rayo is an imprint of HarperCollins Publishers Inc.

Red Midnight
Copyright © 2002 by Ben Mikaelsen

Library of Congress Cataloging-in-Publication Data
Mikaelsen, Ben.
Red midnight / Ben Mikaelsen.
p.   cm.
Summary: After soldiers kill his family, twelve-year-old Santiago and his four-
year-old sister flee Guatemala in a kayak and try to reach the United States.
ISBN 0-380-97745-1 — ISBN 0-06-001228-5 (lib. bdg.)
[1. Guatemala—Fiction. 2. Kayaks and kayaking—Fiction. 3. Survival—
Fiction. 4. Emigration and immigration—Fiction.] I. Title.
PZ7.M5926 Rc 2002   2001039834
[Fic]—dc21   CIP
                                                                         AC

Typography by Andrea Vandergrift
1 2 3 4 5 6 7 8 9 10

First Edition

*This book is dedicated
to all the children of the world
who have seen a red sky
at night.*

CONTENTS

RED
MIDNIGHT

1

SOLDIERS IN THE NIGHT

May 18, 1981
Dos Vías, Guatemala

I TRY TO FORGET the night they burned my village. Those memories are like clouds in my mind. But sometimes the clouds lift, and again I hear screams and soldiers shouting and guns exploding. A dog barks. Another shot echoes, and the dog is quiet. Then there is more shouting and killing.

I remember my mother waking me that night. Fear makes her voice shake as she pushes my little sister into my arms. "Santiago, wake up!" she whispers loudly. "Run! Take Angelina with you. They have come to kill us. Run!"

And my mother is right. As I stumble barefoot toward the trees holding Angelina's hand, soldiers appear behind me. They carry torches that show their laughing faces as they run through our small village burning every home.

Our homes are very simple, with dirt floors, thatch roofs, and walls made of dried cane stalks that burn easily. When families run from the flames, the soldiers kill them. Their guns sound like machetes hitting coconuts.

In the dark, I run hard, pulling Angelina by the hand. But I trip. When I fall, I drag my sister under bushes at the edge of our village. I look back and see the flames, and I see what the soldiers do to my family and to my neighbors.

I have two younger brothers, Arturo and Rolando, and two sisters, Anita and Angelina. I am the oldest, twelve years old. This night, all of my family dies except Angelina. They are all killed as I watch. I see rape and I see torture. I see things happen this night that I can never speak of.

The night is filled with screams of fear and pain. Tears fill my eyes when I see my grandfather, Adolfo, try to run. He is old. I look up at the sky because I cannot watch when they shoot him. Above me the sky is cloudy. A thin moon shines through the clouds like a ghost, and I know that tonight the soldiers do not aim their bullets at the moon.

Angelina clings to me in the dark, and I cover her mouth so she cannot scream. I try to cover her eyes, too, but she will not let me. She knows that something very bad is happening.

Something moves in the bushes near me, and I hold my breath. I think it is a soldier, but a voice that I know whispers very loud, "Santiago, keep running!" It is the voice of my uncle Ramos. He lies near me on the ground. His deep breaths sound like a sick horse when it breathes.

"You must come with us," I say.

"No, I am shot."

"I will help you."

"No," he says. "I am already dead. But you are still alive. Go!"

I nod, but I do not know where a twelve-year-old boy can go with his four-year-old sister. There is no place to run in a country like Guatemala, where everyone is afraid. "Where do we go?" I ask.

"Leave Guatemala. Go as far away as you can and tell what has happened this night."

"But, Uncle, nobody will listen to me. I am only a boy."

Pain makes Uncle Ramos bite his lip until it bleeds. "What you have seen tonight makes you a man," he says, his voice weak. He rolls his body over until he can look into my eyes. "There is a wind that blows and tries to help this country," he says. "Go now! Be part of this wind. You are the only person who can tell of this evil."

"But where can I go?" I ask. "To Mexico?"

Uncle Ramos shakes his head. "There are many soldiers north of here. Go south to Lake Izabal. Take the *cayuco* and sail to the United States of America." Uncle Ramos lifts his chin. "In my pocket, there is my compass.

I have shown you how to use it. Now take it."

I do not argue. The cayuco is a sailing kayak, something Uncle Ramos is very proud of. I reach into his pocket and find the compass. It feels like a large watch.

Uncle Ramos coughs blood from his mouth. "Remember, the red end of the needle always points to the north. Remember that. Now go!"

I let go of Angelina's mouth and stand. As I turn to run, a soldier sees me. The burning flames from the village let him see my face well, and he raises his rifle. I run once more with Angelina into the forest. Behind me the rifle fires again and again. Bullets hit the trees around me like rocks.

I do not stop or look back. Death is as close as my next breath tonight. I run fast into the black night because I know this trail very well. Many times I have carried heavy loads of *maíz* along this trail, from the fields to my village.

"We will find you!" the soldier screams behind me. "Then we will kill you!"

Angelina cannot run anymore and so I carry her. I run even when I cannot breathe, because I am so scared. I do not stop until only the sounds of frogs and crickets fill the night behind me. Then, for the first time, I look back.

The world is not right. Above the trees, I see flames from my village jumping toward the stars. The night sky glows red as if it is burning.

2

THE *CAYUCO*

BEFORE I TELL YOU about my escape and about the cayuco, I must tell you first about myself. My name is Santiago Cruz. The village where I have lived all of my life is called Dos Vías, a small village in the low mountains of Guatemala in Central America. My country is a very great country filled with the stone ruins of my forefathers, the ancient Maya. The old people whisper when they speak of the sacred ruins that reach up through the morning mist, because these places are still sacred.

I have not been to these places. The only place I know far away is the great Lake Izabal. I go to Lake Izabal because my uncle Ramos needs help to harvest his maíz, the corn that we grow to make our tortillas. The mountains where I live are very green and beautiful, with forests so thick that we use machetes to cut our way along the paths. Always we carry machetes, because there are many things in our country that can hurt us.

There are no roads or cars in Dos Vías. We carry water from the streams and we use wood fires to cook. The sides of our mountains have green fields of maíz and forests with many birds, like eagles, parrots, hummingbirds, and owls.

We love this land very much, but because my family is poor, we have only a few chickens and the maíz that we grow. We are campesinos. That means we are country people. Life is hard for all campesinos, but it is even harder for us because we are also *indígenos*, the first people. Our ancestors, the great Maya, lived in this country before the ships came with the Spanish. Even now many Spanish think they are better than us. This I do not understand.

Because walking is the only way to reach our village, we carry everything on our backs. Two times each year my uncle Ramos comes to our village to help us harvest our maíz. That is why my father and I also go to Lake Izabal, where Uncle Ramos lives, to help him with his harvest.

When we go to help Uncle Ramos, we must walk from the mountains for three hours and then ride in the back of a truck for two more hours before we arrive at the *finca*. The finca is the farm where Uncle Ramos lives. Near the finca on Lake Izabal, the cayuco of my uncle Ramos floats beside a small wood dock.

Cayucos are not big white plastic boats like the boats

that tourists use when they visit our country. Those boats are like large buildings that float. No, a cayuco is only a small kayak, a gray dugout boat made from a tree. The cayuco of Uncle Ramos is a sailing kayak as long as a pickup truck, but so narrow that I can reach and hold both sides. The cloth sail looks like the wing of a butterfly and is not very tall. I can reach the top with the paddle.

When I work in the fields with Uncle Ramos picking his maíz, I stand many times to wipe sweat from my forehead. The sun burns like a great ball of fire in the empty sky, and I often stare down at the cool lake and at the cayuco that floats beside the small dock.

This cayuco is not like others that pass along the shore each day while I work. This one has a tall pole in the middle that lifts the sail, which is wrapped around a bottom pole that swings from side to side. I do not ask Uncle Ramos about the cayuco, because my father tells me there is not time for such questions. But I do not need permission to dream. I close my eyes, and I feel like a butterfly with the wind pushing me across the lake.

"Santiago!" shouts my father when he sees me stare at the cayuco during the day. "Work!"

And so I work hard each day. I do not think of the dirt that fills my nose, or the cuts on my hands, or the heat that makes the air like a giant oven. But I cannot stop myself from looking at the little cayuco that sits alone beside the shore. It is as if the cayuco is waiting for me. Maybe it is because my family is so poor, maybe that is why I dream so much of sailing this boat. In my dreams, I am free to drift away like a cloud. But I do not think that such dreams can come true for poor people.

Always when I go home to the mountains, I make small toy cayucos with sails, but they do not work. If the wind blows, my cayucos tip over. One time when Uncle Ramos came to Dos Vías to help us pick maíz, he saw me trying to sail a toy cayuco in a shallow pool by the mountain stream. "This is why your cayuco tips over in the water," he tells me. He helps me to move the sail forward, and he makes the sail so it can move from side to side.

"Where have you learned these things?" I ask.

"I once worked as a fisherman and as a sailor on the Pacific Coast," he explains. "Before the war between the guerrillas and the military began."

"Why do the guerrillas fight the soldiers?" I ask.

"The guerrillas are fighters who say they come to free our country." Uncle Ramos shrugs. "We do not know if that is true."

"Did they make you leave your home?" I ask.

"Not the guerrillas. It is the soldiers who want our land."

"Can they take it?" I ask.

"Oh, yes. The soldiers work for the rich people, *los ricos*. They can do anything they want. They tell us we do not have titles for our land—a piece of paper that proves who is the owner. Well, a title is something many poor campesinos do not know about. The idea of owning land is a strange idea to us, because we do not think that a person can own land. Land belongs to everyone. The earth did not come to us with lines on the ground that said this part is yours and this part is mine. All people are equal. We all help each other and share what we have. This is the only way the indígenos can survive. So why do we need titles?

"Anyway, one day the soldiers come and tell me I will have a title to the land if I sign my fingerprint on a piece of paper. Because I cannot read, I must trust the soldiers. Later I find out I have signed a paper that says I will give away my land. This is the kind of trick that our government plays on poor people who cannot read."

"Why do you not have a family now?" I ask.

Uncle Ramos swallows and looks far across the valley. "They are gone," is all he will say. He takes the toy cayuco from my hands and smiles. "You must learn to read, Santiago. Then you will never do things you do not want to do. Now let me show you how to make your cayuco sail."

That day, Uncle Ramos teaches me why a sailing cayuco is carved different than a regular one. The sharp front and long keel make it more steady passing through large waves. With thin string Uncle Ramos ties the sail so that my toy cayuco crosses the shallow pond sideways to the wind. That for me is like magic. "Teach me more," I beg.

"For that, you must learn to read," Uncle Ramos says again.

"Can you read?" I ask.

Uncle Ramos nods. "Now I can. Losing everything has taught me that all indígena people must learn to read if they want to protect themselves. Our ignorance is our enemy's greatest weapon. Santiago, if you want to learn to read, maybe I can help you."

That night, Uncle Ramos gives me a Spanish magazine about sailing. I hold my breath as I turn each page and stare at the bright-colored pictures of big and beautiful sailboats. All I can do is look at the pictures because I cannot read. But Uncle Ramos begins to teach me the sounds of the letters. Because I speak *Kekchi* like my family, I know very little Spanish. "This is very hard for me," I tell Uncle Ramos.

Uncle Ramos smiles. "Then I must teach you more Spanish. Maybe someday you will go to school." Before I can ask him where, he says, "Do you know that in the United States of America, all children go to school and learn to read and write?"

I shake my head. I do not know these things. It does not seem possible to me.

When Uncle Ramos leaves Dos Vías, I do not forget the things he tells me. I did not know that my ignorance is a weapon to my enemies. Also I think more about sailing. The magazine Uncle Ramos gave me becomes very special, and I guard it like a great treasure because it holds my dreams.

In our village of Dos Vías, there is much work to do. Each day I begin at three in the morning and finish after dark. This does not stop my dreams. After the night's meal is finished, I use my machete to cut myself a strip of *ocote*. Ocote is a part of a pine tree that lights easily and burns very slow. With this for light, I sit against a tree and squint at the sailing pictures because the flame is very dim.

I practice saying the words and sentences Uncle Ramos has taught to me. I know words like *boat* and *sail*. But mostly I look at the pictures in the magazine and dream.

The next time we visit Uncle Ramos to help him harvest his maíz, I want more than anything to sit in his cayuco. I am afraid to ask for this because there is much work to do, but maybe there is a time when I can go to the cayuco by myself.

One night, when I am very tired from a long day of work, I tell my father I want to sleep outside under the sky. "It is too hot to sleep inside," I say.

If my father knows that I lie, he does not say anything. That night, after the breathing of my father and Uncle Ramos changes to snoring, and after the neighbor's dogs stop barking, I stand and walk quietly toward the lake. I follow the fence to where the cattle are kept. The cows shift and moo as they hear me pass in the dark. From there, I follow the road until it reaches the shoreline. Then a rough trail takes me beside the water until I reach the small dock.

In the dark, the sailing cayuco does not look like a butterfly. It looks more like a monster waiting to attack me. I move very slowly now because I am scared. When I step onto the dock, the wood squeaks and it seems loud enough to wake up all the world. I am almost too scared to touch the cayuco, but then I crouch and crawl in. The water splashes against the side as I sit down. I shiver because I am so excited and afraid of what I am doing.

Carefully I lift the paddle and pretend to steer the boat across the waves. I move the paddle out and in, and pretend I am turning. On my right side there is a large board that can be lowered to keep the boat from blowing sideways. I think Uncle Ramos calls this the sideboard. A large pin must be pulled out to let it swing into the water on a big metal bolt. I reach and pull the pin. The board splashes down and I turn in the dark to see if anybody hears me.

Next I follow every rope with my fingers until I know where each one goes and what each one does. For a very long time, I sit in the dark and pretend to sail across the ocean. In my mind I sail over waves as big as hills. I dare to do many things that night, but I do not dare to raise the sail. It is tied to the swinging sail poles with pieces of rope.

Finally, when I am so tired my head nods, I stand to climb from the cayuco.

"Are you afraid to raise the sail?" a deep voice asks from the dark.

3

LEARNING TO SAIL

I TURN AS IF LIGHTNING has hit my body. At the end of the dock stands Uncle Ramos. He is watching me with clear dark eyes. How long he has watched me I do not know.

"I am sorry, Uncle," I say. My words shake with fear as I jump from the cayuco.

Uncle Ramos waits for me in the dark. "If you want to know how to sail my cayuco, why don't you ask me?" he says.

"Because maybe that will make you mad," I say.

"And I am not mad to find you here alone without my permission?" Uncle Ramos asks. His voice sounds like the growl of a dog.

"You can punish me," I say.

He stares at me, and then in the moonlight he smiles. "I think your heart has stopped beating. That is enough punishment," he says. Then he asks me, "Do you want to learn to sail this cayuco?"

My ears cannot believe what they hear. "Yes," I say. "More than anything else I know."

"Okay," he says. "If we finish gathering the maíz by Sunday, I will teach you how to sail. Now it is too dark to pick my nose."

I laugh, but I am still afraid. "How much do you use this cayuco?" I ask.

As we walk Uncle Ramos talks. "I do not use the cayuco very much except to take maíz down the Río Dulce to Puerto Barrios. But this boat is a good boat and can sail the ocean if that is what I need. It is made from a big *guanacaste* tree that I cut from the forest myself. The guanacaste tree is the best tree a person can use. It is strong and straight and does not rot easily in water."

"How far can you sail with this sailing cayuco?" I ask.

"To any place where there is wind and water," he says. "To Honduras, Belize, the Yucatán, Cuba, or even the United States of America."

"The United States of America," I say, shaking my head. "I do not know how far that is, but it must be a very long sail."

Uncle Ramos walks fast toward home as he speaks. "Yes, it is a very long sail and a very dangerous sail."

"My father will be mad if he knows I have come here tonight without permission," I say.

"Then maybe that is something we should not tell him," Uncle Ramos answers.

"Thank you," I say quietly.

When we reach the home of Uncle Ramos, I try to be quiet when I carry my woven *petate* inside to sleep. I think my father hears me, but he does not say anything.

All of that week I work harder than I have ever worked in my life. The nights do not let me sleep well because I am thinking about learning to sail the cayuco.

When Sunday finally comes, I cannot remember my own name because I am so excited. Very early in the morning, we gather fruit and make tortillas to eat during our sail. I think my father is excited, too, but he does not show it.

That day, when Uncle Ramos takes us out to sail, he teaches me how to raise and lower the sail and how to change direction. He teaches me to empty water, to understand the wind, and to sail with bad weather. He even teaches me how to sail against the wind. This is something that my mind does not understand.

"How do you sail to the United States of America?" I ask.

Uncle Ramos pulls a small map from his pocket, then squints across the lake and points. "First you sail to that island over there. I call it the Island of the Birds because so many of them nest there. From there you go under a big bridge by the city of Fronteras. That takes you to another lake called El Golfete. When you reach the other end of El Golfete, you enter a river called the Río Dulce. This turns and bends through deep gorges until you pass a big Spanish fort on your left. There you enter the Gulf of Honduras and the Caribbean Sea."

"Then do you reach the United States of America?" I ask.

Uncle Ramos laughs hard. "No, you still have not left Guatemala. Now you sail north." He unfolds the map to show me. "During the day you must keep the morning sun on your right and the evening sun on your left. At night you follow the North Star. Tonight I will show you that star and how you can always find it."

Pointing along the shore going north on the map, Uncle Ramos explains, "There is a strong current called the Gulf Current that helps you to sail north. The trip is very dangerous because there are storms and pirates. There are sharks longer than the cayuco, and the sun is so hot it can cook an egg."

"But then you reach the United States of America?" I ask.

Uncle Ramos shakes his head. "After you sail north for maybe a week, you are not able to follow land anymore. When the land disappears to the west, you are at the top of the Yucatán. Now begins the most dangerous part of the trip. The current will push you hard to the east, but you must always keep sailing north."

Uncle Ramos points at the map again. "If you keep sailing across the Gulf of Mexico, you will reach land somewhere along here." He points to a coast of the United States. "The United States of America has many small regions called states. Where you will land is called Florida."

"How do you know all this?" I ask.

Uncle Ramos does not answer this question.

"How long does it take to sail to Florida?" I ask.

Uncle Ramos looks at the map and thinks. "Maybe twenty days."

"What happens if you do not keep sailing north when you cross the Gulf?" I ask.

"If the current takes you east between Cuba and Florida, you will drift into the Atlantic Ocean. If that happens you will die. The ocean is not like your parents," he says. I see Uncle Ramos wink at my father. "The ocean does not forgive you when you disobey or make mistakes."

It is after this visit to Uncle Ramos that the bad stories first come to Dos Vías. The stories are sent from other villages higher in the mountains and tell of much fighting between the guerrillas and the military soldiers. The stories tell of villages burned, people tortured, and thousands killed or left without a home. I do not think these stories can be true. How can you kill a thousand people? But my father tells me the soldiers can do these things.

Soon the guerrillas come to our village. At first it is

only to ask questions and to ask for food. It is hard for me to know if they are friends or enemies. The guerrillas say they fight for the rights of the indígenos and the poor campesinos like us. But I can see fear in the eyes of my mother and father when they bow their heads and give food to the guerrillas.

When the military soldiers come into Dos Vías, I see that my parents are even more afraid. The soldiers ask many questions, and they wave their rifles and shout, "Anybody who helps the guerrillas will be shot!"

Now this is a problem. Maybe if we help the soldiers, we will die. Maybe if we help the guerrillas, we will die. Always we are afraid of death. We do not want to die. We want only to live and to grow our maíz. This is all that we want. We do not think the bullets from a guerrilla's gun hurt any less than the bullets from a soldier's gun. A bullet is a bullet.

There is another problem. In every village in the world, I think there are neighbors who do not like each other. After the soldiers and the guerrillas come, some people say their neighbor is helping the other side. Soon everybody thinks somebody else is a spy.

In Dos Vías my mother and father are liked very much. Mother tells everyone that we must help each other. I hear my father say, "If enough people hope and dream and fight for what we know is right, Guatemala can change, even for us, the poor campesinos indígenos."

Me, I do not know if what they say can be true, but I

think it is true that people need hope. I know the indígenos in my village had some hope. They believed in their hearts that someday they, too, could be free and live without fear.

But the night when the soldiers burned Dos Vías, that night, hope died along with all of my people. When the blood dried on the ground, the hearts of the indígenos died with their bodies. I will always remember that night as the night of evil, and I will always think of that night as the night that God turned his back on the indígenos. Yes, he turned his back on us.

4

COCONUTS IN LOS SANTOS

THE NIGHT THEY KILLED MY FAMILY, after Uncle Ramos tells me to run, I keep running into the night. Angelina is scared and tired, so again I carry her until I come to the field where my family grows maíz for the tortillas we eat. Now I must stop.

Ahead in the dark a horse stands with a broken rope hanging from its neck. His head is up and his eyes stare at me with fear. He does not know what is walking toward him in the night. I move forward very slow with my hand out. I click my tongue and pretend I have maíz to feed him. The horse lets me take the rope and tie a loop around his nose like a halter. Angelina does not let go of my leg.

There is little time, but I kneel beside Angelina. I look into her scared face and make myself smile. "Do you want to go for a ride on a horse?" I ask.

She blinks her big eyes and nods.

"Do you want to go as fast as the wind?"

I think I see her smile in the dark.

"Good," I say. "But you must hold on. Can you hold on very tight?"

Again Angelina nods.

"Okay, we are ready." There is no saddle, so I jump onto the horse's back and pull Angelina up behind me. I turn the horse down the mountain, click my tongue, and slap the halter rope. The horse leaps ahead into a gallop.

Angelina holds on tightly. "Go slower!" she screams.

"We must go as fast as the wind!" I call back.

At night it is easy to fall, and riding this fast is foolish. But tonight I have no choice. Even now maybe the soldiers follow us. I let the horse decide where to go. It is safer this way.

Our horse is not a fat horse, and the bone from his back is like a board bouncing under us. "Ouch!" screams Angelina. "Ouch!" She begins to cry.

More rifle shots echo behind me in the night, but I do not look back. We ride hard until there is nothing behind us but a dark quiet sky. Finally I slow. Soon we will come to the village of Los Santos. I know people there, and maybe it will be a safe place. If I can stay with friends of my father, I will not have to go to Lake Izabal. Lake Izabal is very far away, and I am tired. Also I am very scared.

Angelina's arms grow tired and she almost falls off. I

reach back and pull her around in front of me. With one arm I hold her. She stops crying.

When we reach the hill above Los Santos, I am very tired and weak. My muscles ache and the skin on the inside of my legs burns. I have the hair on the horse's neck wrapped tight around my fingers. It is good to see the small fires from the village below.

"Can we stop now?" Angelina asks, her voice scared. "Where are we?"

"Yes, we can stop riding now," I say. "That is Los Santos." I jump off the horse and lift Angelina to the ground.

"Did we go as fast as the wind?" she asks.

I smile. "Angelina, we went faster than the wind."

As I walk into the village of Los Santos, I lead the horse and hold Angelina's hand. Something is very wrong. I know this when I find cane stalks and boards burning on the ground. This is all that is left of Los Santos. All the homes are burned down the same as in Dos Vías, and a very bad smell fills the air.

In the dark there is something else that is wrong. There are no people, and on the ground between the burned homes there are coconuts. I pick up a burning piece of wood and hold it in front of me. Now I can see better. I reach down and pick up a coconut. Suddenly the air stops in my chest. I drop the coconut and grab Angelina's hand again. I know now why the air has a bad smell.

"Where are the people?" Angelina asks quietly.

"They are gone. All gone," I whisper. I do not tell Angelina that the coconuts we see are the skulls of people who are burned. "We must go," I say. "We must ride the horse again."

I hold the burning wood over my head. Now I can see dead bodies near the trees that are not burned. There are men and women and old people and children. All of them shot. I am almost to the edge of the village when a body in the tall grass makes me trip. I fall onto the body. Angelina falls with me and screams. When I stand, I am shaking. It is Carlos.

Carlos is a boy who has come with his family to our village. He is my age, and many times we have kicked a football to each other. Carlos kicked a football very hard. Tonight his legs are cut off and they lie beside him in the grass. I shake my head hard from side to side to make this bad dream go away, but the body of Carlos does not go away. I put my hand over Angelina's eyes, but already she has seen too much. Her body is shaking.

I stand and stare at the legs beside Carlos. Those are the same legs that kicked a ball to me many times. What did those legs do wrong? Those legs did not belong to a guerrilla or to a soldier. They belonged to only a young boy. I know the soldiers have done this, because already this night I have seen how they kill.

I do not understand the soldiers. When they ask our people, "Are you communist?" we do not understand them. The indígenos want to live without fear. They want to grow their maíz and teach their children respect for the ways of the ancients, *los ancianos.*

My parents always told me that we must help others and be good to the world around us. If a soldier is hurt, we must help him. If a guerrilla is hurt, we must also help him. I think this is why the soldiers call us communists. But I think that helping people just makes us good people, not communists.

If I am something, I am indígeno, and I have in me the spirit and the blood of the ancient Maya. That is what I am. When I die my body does not die less from the bullet of a soldier's gun or the bullet of a guerrilla's gun. Death is death.

But I am alive, and I do not understand. All the people of my village have died with only machetes and sticks in their hands. How can the soldiers be afraid of this? The priest tells me I am a child of God. But if this is true, where is God tonight when all of his children are killed? I do not think that God would watch so many of his children be tortured and raped and killed. He did not see my mother and father and my brothers and my sister die. Tonight everyone has died except for Angelina. And my friend, Carlos, he is dead, too. His legs are cut off. God did not see this. I am the only one who has seen this, I think.

No, if there is a God, then tonight I think he is like the soldiers and does not care about us. He does not care about the poor campesinos from the mountains who do not have money to wear fancy clothes or to shine their shoes. Things have happened this night that even the sky and the wind should never see. I understand now why Uncle Ramos has told me to run so far away. It is because here in Guatemala, there is not a God to protect us. That is why Uncle Ramos has told me to tell what I see. This is something the living can still do.

And so I kneel once again beside Angelina. "Look into my eyes," I tell her. She tries to look away but I hold her head. "Look into my eyes," I tell her again.

And now she looks.

"Do you want to go far away from here and ride on a boat with a sail?"

Angelina nods.

"We will be sailors," I say.

"What is a sailor?" Angelina asks.

I do not know what to tell her, because I know we are not sailors. We are only two foolish and scared children.

5

PIGS IN THE *MAÍZ*

WHEN WE RIDE the horse away from Los Santos, my mind is numb. I tell myself I must be careful. I must be awake when I ride. Even at night there are guerrillas and soldiers on these paths. So I make the horse walk. My ears listen to every sound the night makes.

From here it will take one hour of riding to reach the town of Chollo. That is where I must leave the horse and find a truck that goes to Lake Izabal.

I feel sorry for Angelina. Her young mind does not yet understand what has happened. I know I will need to explain this night to her sometime, but tonight I am not sure I understand myself what has happened.

We ride on narrow paths across many fields, through valleys, and across steep ridges. Angelina taps my shoulder. "I want to go home," she says.

I think carefully before I tell her, "We are going

home." This is true, because when you have no home, any place new can be home.

When I think we cannot ride the bony horse another step, I hear the sound of dance music. Ahead is Chollo, a busy town with electricity, cars, much noise, and garbage in the streets. Even in the middle of the night, there is the noise of trucks and music. Before I see the lights, I smell the smoke of motors.

It is too far to ride a horse from here to Lake Izabal, so before I reach Chollo, I get off and help Angelina to the ground. I wrap the halter rope around the horse's neck so it will not tangle, then I slap the horse hard and he gallops into the dark. He will make some lucky person a good horse.

After the horse disappears, I hope I have done what is right. It is too dark to look at the compass in my pocket, but I look up at the sky and find the North Star. That is the star that Uncle Ramos has told me will lead a sailor to the United States of America. Tonight the star must stay behind me if I want to go south and find Lake Izabal.

We do not have any money to ride a bus, and it is very dangerous to travel alone in the middle of the night with a little sister. All that I can do is wait near the *restaurante* on the edge of Chollo. Here the trucks stop for food. I must find a truck to hide in.

I watch as a truck stops that has wood stacked high. The next truck has many chickens in cages. I let myself think that maybe Angelina and I can ride with the chickens, but then I think, no, Angelina will cry. Two buses go past. And then a truck stops that is carrying dried cobs of maíz. A canvas tarp covers the truck's big box.

"Do you want to go ride with some maíz?" I ask Angelina.

"I want to go home," she says stubbornly. Her bottom lip sticks out when she speaks like this.

"I think if you ride with me in the maíz, we will find home," I tell her.

Slowly Angelina lets me lead her through the shadows of the buildings until we are close to the truck. I kneel beside Angelina. "Listen very carefully," I tell her. "I need to go make room in the maíz. You wait here until I am ready. When I wave to you, run to me. Okay?"

She nods.

"Stay right here until you see me wave," I say again more strongly.

Again she nods, and I let go of her hand. There is nobody in the street, so I run fast across the dim road until the shadow of the truck hides me. I look back, and Angelina waits patiently. Quickly I crawl up on the truck and pull the tarp to one side. The back is almost filled with dried cobs of maíz but there is room to ride. I turn and wave for Angelina to come.

She sees me and starts to walk toward the truck. When she is halfway across the street, a man walks around the corner of the building. I whisper very loud to

Angelina, "Hurry!" but she stops and stares at the person. "Come!" I whisper, as loud as I dare.

But Angelina stands and watches the man, who is drunk. He carries a bottle in his hand and stumbles as he walks. He stops and looks at Angelina with glassy eyes. I run to the middle of the street and grab Angelina's hand. She is scared as I pull her across the street. "We must hurry or we cannot ride with the maíz," I tell her. Quickly I lift her high into the back of the truck, then crawl up myself and pull the tarp back over us.

We wait quietly in the dark. It is hard to breathe, but Angelina does not complain. "It is like we are hiding," she says, her voice filled with mischief.

I smile in the dark. "Yes, it is like we are hiding," I whisper. "So we must be quiet."

We wait a long time. This is something that is very hard for a little girl. I am almost ready to lift the tarp for some fresh air when I hear the driver open the door and climb in. The motor starts. A loud grinding sound makes the truck jerk forward, and then we pull onto the dirt road. Soon wind blows under the tarp, and the dust from the road and the maíz makes us close our eyes. Because of the wind and engine noise, I dare talk to Angelina.

"Nobody else is lucky enough to ride with us in this truck of maíz," I tell her. My words hold a sad truth.

"I am hungry," she says.

"You are so lucky," I tell her. I push my hand through the maíz until I find a cob that is not as dry as the rest.

"Here," I say, putting it in her hands.

"I want tortillas and frijoles," she says.

"Let me look," I say. I pretend to dig into the maíz again to look. I shake my head. "The last people who rode with the maíz have eaten all the tortillas and frijoles. They must be pigs not to leave some for my sister, Angelina."

Angelina giggles. "Pigs in the maíz," she says. "We will make up a song called 'Pigs in the Maíz.'"

And so we make up a song. Angelina sings as she chews on the cob. Each time the truck slows, I place my fingers gently over her mouth. I do not have to press hard. She has learned now she must be quiet.

"I am thirsty," she says.

Again I pretend to look through the maíz. "You know what?" I say, acting surprised.

"I know, I know," she says. "The pigs drank everything, too."

I lift the tarp a little to look outside when we go through each town. Some towns I remember and some I do not. I remember Boca del Monte. Later maybe it is La Cumbre and San Pedro Cadenas that we pass. The road is very dusty and I pull my shirt over my mouth. Angelina uses her dirty red dress to cover her mouth.

Late in the night the road to Lake Izabal becomes black tar and there is not so much dust. Angelina falls asleep. I am glad for her. I wish that I, too, could fall asleep this night. I did not know that when the sun went down yesterday, by morning all of my family would be gone except Angelina. And now I am in a truck of maíz near Lake Izabal. Our world has changed so much. My father was right when he told me that changes do not always ask our permission.

When we pass the town of Semax, I know that Lake Izabal is close. I watch carefully now because we must jump from the truck before it stops in the big city called Fronteras. From there another road leaves and follows the shore around the lake. In cities there are many lights and I know somebody might see us. I let Angelina sleep more. She will need all the sleep she can find.

Me, I am not so tired, but I feel empty inside and I feel very old. I pull the tarp back and lift my head to look forward. The lights of Fronteras shine ahead. This night scares me. What if somebody sees us when we enter the city? What if they catch Angelina and me? What will they do to us?

I wake Angelina up. "Now is the most exciting part of our ride," I tell her. "If we get down from the truck of maíz after it stops, it will be boring. So I think we should jump off when it is still moving, okay?"

She rubs at her sleepy eyes with the back of her tight fists and looks forward into the wind. The city is closer now. I keep looking ahead. We cannot jump going this fast, so I wait. When the truck begins to slow, it shifts gears. The engine growls. As we enter Fronteras I see only two people walking beside the road because it is very late in the night.

I wait for the truck to slow just a little more, and then I throw back the tarp all the way. I grab Angelina by the waist and lift her over the edge. I hold her under one arm as I crawl down the back of the truck to where I can jump. I hope the truck driver does not see me.

Angelina holds my neck so tight that it is hard to breathe. This is okay because I am all she has to hold on to.

Then I jump.

I try to land on my feet but we are going too fast. We fall hard. Angelina lands on top of me and does not hit the road, but I lose the air in my chest and scrape skin from my arm and shoulder. For a little time I lie still and hope I have not broken a bone. Then Angelina asks, "Can we do that again?"

I stand and hope the driver does not see us in his mirror. "I'm sorry, we can only do that once," I tell Angelina. Quickly I take her hand and cross the street. My arm and shoulder burn with pain, but after what has happened this night, the pain is nothing.

Angelina turns and waves good-bye to the truck.

"Who did you wave to?" I ask.

"To the pigs in the maíz," she answers.

6

MUD IN THE GAS TANK

I AM NOT SURE what time it is as I stand on the street of
Fronteras holding Angelina's hand. This night is like a
long black cave that has no end. The roosters crow, so it
cannot be long before the sun rises. I know we are in
great danger if we are still in the city when morning
comes. Soldiers hunt down and kill people who have
seen what they do.

Quickly I walk three blocks to where the road enters
the city from Lake Izabal. No trucks drive the road this
early, but this is the road that will take me to the home
of Uncle Ramos thirty kilometers away. I see only skinny
stray dogs digging through the garbage that is everywhere in this place. This city has smoke and garbage and
truck motors. These things hide the sounds and the
smells of the forest.

Angelina walks by my side. Her big eyes stare away

into the dark as if she is lost or dazed. Maybe she is both. Her long black hair is matted and tangled. We walk along the road until I see a pickup truck parked in front of a house. There are tall sides on the pickup made of tree branches, like a cage without a top. The motor still runs, so maybe the driver will be back soon. I do not know if he goes to Lake Izabal, but the pickup faces that direction. I walk Angelina across the street near the pickup and we stand in the dark shadows waiting.

We do not stand there long before a truck comes toward us. Good, I think. Maybe we can ride in this truck. But when the truck slows, I see it is filled with soldiers. It is easy to see the soldiers because there is light in the street and they are standing up in the back of the truck like cows. Maybe these are the same soldiers that attacked Dos Vías. The truck stops very close to us, close enough that I can see their faces. The soldiers begin to climb out.

I do not have time to think. I know only that very soon one of them will see us. Maybe they will know who we are. As fast as I can, I lift Angelina into the back of the pickup and crawl in behind her. "Lie down," I tell her. There is no time to make up a nice story, so I hold my hand over her mouth.

I do not know what we lie on, only that it is soft and wet. And then I smell horse dung. I know now that the pickup has hauled many horses. There is nothing I can do. The soldiers are walking toward us. Their loud voices complain about the night and about their long ride. I think I hear one soldier say something about Dos Vías.

Now they walk beside the pickup. I do not dare breathe. If even one soldier looks through the branches into the pickup, he will see us. I hope that Angelina does not move.

Now I am glad for the darkness. I think something protects us because soon the voices of the soldiers pass. Very soon I hear the driver of the pickup come out from the house and crawl into the front. He drives away from the house fast. He looks many times over his shoulder at the soldiers. I think that maybe he is afraid, too. That is why he does not see us. He keeps driving toward Lake Izabal.

"We are lying in mud," Angelina whispers to me. "Like pigs."

"Yes," I say. "Like pigs." I do not want Angelina to get up or place her face in the horse dung, so I say, "We will roll over and look up at the stars."

As we lie on our backs and stare at the sky, I feel something wrong with the pickup. It speeds up, then slows down, and then swerves left and right on the road. I think maybe the driver is drunk.

"Why do we keep turning?" Angelina asks. "It makes me sick."

"The man is a very nice man," I say. "He tries to make our ride more fun."

"You smell like a horse," she says.

I smile and watch the stars swing back and forth above me in the sky. "Yes," I say. "I smell like a horse and so do you because we have been riding a horse tonight." I hope she does not ask about the horse dung under us.

The pickup keeps turning and swaying and soon I, too, feel sick. I sit up to breathe fresh air, then I must crawl to the back to throw up again and again onto the passing road. When I lie down once more, I look to make sure the driver has not seen me, then I look over at Angelina and see that she is falling asleep.

Angelina has a gentle look on her small face, a look that tells me her thoughts are good. I do not know how this can be, after what has happened. I wish that I, too, could fall asleep and forget the bad. But there are many things to wish for. I wish the driver was not drunk. I wish my horse ride down from the mountains with Angelina was only for fun. More than anything I wish that the gunshots from this night were only firecrackers. If these things could be true, then maybe this night would be only a dream.

Until now the night has given me only time to escape and take care of Angelina. There has been no time to think about myself. Now with stars looking down at me, I have time to think of what has happened and it scares me. All of my life my mother has told me, "Santiago, you are very big and very handsome. You are braver than any boy in Dos Vías."

I think now that she is wrong. Tonight I feel very

small and I want to hide. Many bad things have happened that should not happen to people. This night has known much fear, and it is not over. Still I must get Angelina off this pickup and into the home of Uncle Ramos before there is light.

I am not sure I remember where Uncle Ramos lived. When I traveled with my father, I was looking around me at everything that was new. I was not thinking, "Okay, here we must turn this way or now we must turn that way." But now I am scared. Why did I not watch better? Maybe already we have gone too far. What if this drunk driver takes me to a different place I do not know? What if he crashes?

I stare out the side of the pickup into the night to find where I am. Many fields, homes, and buildings pass us. I do not remember any of them, but a dim moonlight shines on the lake. It makes me feel good. If I take the road too far, I know it will go away from the lake.

For many kilometers we travel. The driver keeps turning and changing his speed. Two times we almost go off the road. Maybe he is falling asleep. I decide I must get Angelina out of this pickup even if we do not reach the home of Uncle Ramos. Here in Guatemala many people die in accidents because of bad roads and because of drinking. But how do I make the driver stop? I look around me and try to think. The long night makes my thoughts numb.

In the dark we pass a waterfall near the road, and

suddenly I remember. There is a waterfall on the road not far from the home of Uncle Ramos. This I do remember. Now I must stop the pickup fast, but how? If I throw horse dung over the front onto the windshield, maybe the driver will stop, but he will catch us. A flat tire will stop him, but I cannot think how to make a tire lose air. All I have is a pickup full of horse dung and very little time.

Then I think of another idea. I stay low and crawl carefully to the back. I reach my hand out between the branches and feel along the side of the pickup for the cap where gas is added. The driver swerves again. This time he almost leaves the road. This wakes Angelina. She looks around and sees me reaching outside the pickup.

I hold my finger to my mouth, then wave my hand for her to crawl to my side. As she reaches my side, I find the gas cap and twist it off. I hand the cap to Angelina. "Hold this," I whisper. I pick up a handful of horse dung and push it into the gas hole. As I reach for more, Angelina whispers, "What are you doing?"

"I am putting mud in the gas tank."

Angelina watches me with big tired eyes. "Why?"

"Because it is time to stop, and I do not think a motor runs very well on mud," I whisper.

I stuff many handfuls of horse dung in the tank and wait for the motor to stop. Angelina reaches down with her little fingers and gives me more horse dung. I smile. "Thank you," I say. I do not know very much about motors, but a motor cannot run very long with horse dung in the gas. Then, like a shadow, the road into the home of Uncle Ramos passes us in the night.

I work faster, and the pickup swerves more. Angelina hands me horse dung so fast she starts to throw it at me and giggle. I point at the driver and put a finger to my lips again.

Suddenly the motor coughs and slows. I stuff one more handful of dung into the tank for good luck, then I grab Angelina's hand and pull her under my arm so I am ready to jump.

"Can we jump again?" Angelina asks.

I nod as the motor coughs harder and the pickup slows. "But be quiet," I tell Angelina. "If you are very quiet, I will jump out of the back again."

As the pickup rolls to a stop, I jump, holding Angelina by the waist under one arm. I land on my feet and run fast into the night, away from the pickup and back toward the home of Uncle Ramos. My family is too poor to wear shoes, and so my feet have become very tough. Still the gravel hurts my feet when I run. Behind us the engine coughs one last time and then quits. I lower Angelina to the ground and we run some more.

When we stop to let Angelina rest, I hear the drunk driver behind us swearing very loudly. I wonder what he will do when the sun comes up and he finds what has happened? I think this drunk man will grow very old and still not know how horse dung filled his gas tank. But maybe what I did this night has saved his life.

The crickets have stopped making their noise, and the stars above me have grown dim when I finally reach the road that leads to where Uncle Ramos once lived. Now it is only one kilometer more. I walk fast because everywhere in this country there are eyes that can see us and tell the soldiers. We do not stop except to go to the bathroom.

At last, in the gray morning darkness, we find the small hut, made with slabs of wood and palm leaves for a roof. There is a door with wire wrapped around a nail to keep out the dogs and chickens. I unwrap the wire. Then we are safely inside, and I close the door. Standing in the dark, it is as if a weight greater than the whole world has lifted from my body.

"We made it, Angelina," I say with a tired voice.

"I did not have fun when you jumped," she says.

"Why?" I ask.

She giggles. "Because we did not fall over."

I hug Angelina, and I laugh, maybe because I have been so scared during the night. "Next time we will fall over," I promise her.

It is too dark to see around the small room, so I feel with my hands until I find Uncle Ramos's bed. In our village of Dos Vías always we sleep on the ground on *petates*, woven grass mats. My mother taught me that the earth is our true mother and that we must be close to her. Because of this we do not use chairs. At home we sit and eat on petates and we sleep on petates. Why should we be far from our mother?

But now I am more tired than I have ever been, and I find no petates. I do not think it will hurt to sleep one night on a soft mattress. Mother Earth will understand. I lead Angelina to the bed. "We will sleep here," I say.

"Okay," she says, and crawls onto the bed in the dark.

I lie down, too tired to think.

"Here," Angelina says, tapping my side.

"What?" I ask, forcing my eyes open.

She holds out her hand. I feel for her hand in the dark. In her small fingers she is still holding the gas cap.

7

THE HOME
OF UNCLE RAMOS

ALONE WITH ANGELINA in the home of Uncle Ramos, I
sleep hard. My sleep is the sleep of the dead, except the
dead do not dream. I dream of many things of which I
am afraid—soldiers and guns and rich people who do
not care what happens to poor campesinos and poor
indígenos. In my dreams I hear guns and I try to run. The
soldiers catch me, and one raises his rifle to shoot me.
Above me the sky burns, and then I wake up with sweat
wetting my face and body. I do not know where I am,
and it takes time to remember.

Beside me Angelina sleeps the sleep of angels. I do
not know how this can be. She has seen all that I have
seen, but moonlight through the window lets me see the
thin smile that lifts her lips. She cuddles close to my
side, and her little round face is like a smiling moon. I
love my sister. She is all that is left of my family. She is

the only thing now that I can trust. She does not hurt me or scare me.

The next time I wake up the sun is high in the sky and a strong hand is shaking my shoulder. "What are you doing here?" shouts a loud voice. I open my eyes, and a large old man is standing above me, a machete in his hand. I move to get up and run, but he waves the machete over my head. "What are you doing here?" he shouts again.

Angelina wakes up, and I pull her close. "Uncle Ramos has told me to come here," I say, choking on my words.

The man stares at me. "Ramos is your uncle?"

I nod.

"Why does he tell you to come here?" the man asks.

I do not dare say anything more. "Who are you?" I ask.

The man waves his machete over his shoulder toward the door. "I live one kilometer down the shore, but I watch this land when Ramos is gone." Still the man looks at me with eyes that tell me I have done something wrong.

"Where is Ramos?" he asks.

I stare at the old man. His clothes are like rags on his body from working the fields. The hot sun has made his skin as rough and worn as leather. Slowly he lowers his machete, and the angry look leaves his eyes.

Because he is also a poor campesino, I tell him about

the soldiers and the killing. I tell him about riding into Los Santos and finding everyone dead. Sadness fills my eyes with tears and I begin to cry, but still I keep talking. "The truck of maíz carried us to Fronteras, and then a drunk driver in a pickup has brought us here," I say. I decide not to tell about the horse dung in the gas tank.

When I finish the man puts his machete on the bed and places one hand on my shoulder and one hand on Angelina's little head. His eyes, too, have filled with tears. "*Madre de Dios*," he whispers, looking up to heaven. "Is it true what you tell me?"

I nod.

"It is very dangerous for you to be here," he says. "We also have many soldiers."

"Uncle Ramos has taught me how to use his sailing cayuco," I say. "He has told me to take the cayuco and to sail far away and tell the world what I have seen."

"Where will you sail to?" the man asks.

"To the United States of America," I say.

"With your sister?"

I nod.

The man stares at us for a long time to let his mind think. "Let me go and have my wife make you food," he says. "I will come back, and then we will talk. There are many things I must tell you."

As the man stands, he holds out his hand. "My name is Enrique."

I shake his hand. "My name is Santiago. This is my

sister, Angelina. Do you have any water?" I ask.

Enrique nods. "I will bring you water now before I leave, but do not go outside. If anyone learns there are strangers here, the soldiers will come."

Soon Enrique returns with a big pail of water. "Remember, do not go outside," he tells me.

After Enrique leaves I hold Angelina. "How are you?" I ask.

She looks out the window. "I think we have played enough," she says. "It is time to go home. I want to see Mama and Papa."

I know that Angelina has seen everyone killed and our home burned. But I think that her mind is pretending these things have not happened. It is okay that she pretends, but I do not know if I should help her to pretend. "You know something very bad has happened," I say. "We cannot go home now. You will have to be a very brave girl because we must sail to a place far away."

"Where do we go?" she asks.

"The United States of America. It is a place with much food, many toys, and many little cats and dogs." I say this because I know Angelina likes cats and dogs very much.

Angelina's eyes fill with tears. "I want to go home," she says again, her quiet little voice filled with hurt.

I hug Angelina. "Don't cry, Angel," I say. "Someday things will be better." This is a promise I must believe myself.

Angelina does not cry loud and angry like many children. I think she is the bravest girl that I know. She wipes at her eyes and tries to smile.

"Are you thirsty?" I ask.

Angelina nods.

I find cups and we drink much water. We are also very hungry but there is no food. So we sleep more.

When we wake up from this sleep, the sun is low in the sky. As I wait for Enrique, I take water and wash Angelina's face and hands. I also use water to clean the shoulder I hurt when I jumped off the truck. The scraped skin is red and still bleeds.

Finally there are footsteps. I put my fingers on Angelina's lips so she knows to be quiet. The steps come to the door, then a quiet voice says, "Hello, we are back." The door opens, and Enrique enters. Behind him walks a woman with a bundle in her arms. She is old and thin and looks tired, as if she is sick. "This is Silvia," he says.

Angelina smiles to see a woman. I think the woman reminds her of our mother.

We say hello, and the woman unwraps her bundle. "Here is some food," she says.

Angelina reaches for the food before the bundle is open, and the woman smiles. "Enrique has told me what happened to you," she says. "We are poor, but we will help you all that we can."

As Angelina and I eat tortillas and fruit, Enrique speaks to us. "I have known Ramos for many years. All of our lives there have been bad things that happen to the indígenos. Ramos built his cayuco not to carry maíz to the market but to someday sail away from Guatemala. That was his dream. He wanted to go to where people could speak without fear. He wanted to tell the world of the evil that is here in Guatemala. Silvia and I are the only ones who know this. Now, if he is dead, he has given his dream to you.

"We have heard the stories of villages being burned in the mountains. Even here there are killings. Every day people disappear. We hear of many thousands who try to leave Guatemala and go as refugees to Mexico."

"Do they make it?" I ask.

Enrique shrugs. "Some do, but many die. There is not enough food, and many people get sick. They vomit and have fever and diarrhea. What you do is what many indígenos wish to do. If you can go to the United States of America, there is hope."

"But what if we die?" I ask.

Enrique is quiet before he speaks. "Here we live like animals. Maybe it is better to drown than to die by a bullet. Maybe it is better to end your life fast on the ocean than to die slowly from cholera, malaria, amoebas, and starvation. Here we have no hope. If you try to sail the cayuco to the United States, at least you will sail with hope."

"Maybe things will get better here," I say.

Enrique shakes his head. "The rich people do not

care. For years we try to tell them that we, the indígenos, also have feelings and hope. All we want is to live like humans."

"Why does that make us the enemy?" I ask.

"Because the rich have no conscience."

"Do you think we can make it to the United States of America?" I ask.

Enrique nods. "If we were younger, maybe Silvia and I would go with you, but we are old and Silvia is sick from a mosquito bite that carries a disease. I have thought much since I found you today. You must leave as soon as you can."

"Tonight?" I ask.

Enrique nods. "Yes, tonight," he says. "I have sailed this cayuco many times, so I will sail with you until you reach the open Gulf. There are many things I can show you that will help you. When we reach the ocean, I will get off at the shore and come back here on a bus. Then you will be alone. If there is good weather, I think you might be okay."

"What if there is bad weather?" I ask.

Enrique shakes his head. "If the weather is very bad, you must try to find an island or go to shore."

I have many questions but Enrique keeps talking. "When you sail the coast north, you must not stop unless you find an empty island," Enrique says. "Everywhere there are people who can rob you, kill you, or tell the soldiers. We will send food with you. It is not very much, but it will help to keep you alive.

"Here," he says, giving me a machete. "You will need this to break coconuts, cut fruit, kill fish, and to fix the boat. Use it also to protect yourself."

"Why do you do all this for us?" I ask.

Enrique's wife, Silvia, has spoken little until now. She kneels beside us and puts her hand on Angelina's head. "Ramos has helped Enrique and me very much. After he lost his family, he was like a brother to us."

"How did he lose his family?" I ask.

Silvia does not answer this question either. "Here in Guatemala you and your sister are in great danger," she says. "Enrique and I have talked many times of escaping, but it is only a dream. We are too old, and I am sick. No, we cannot go, but you can.

"If you try to make it to the United States of America, you will carry all of our dreams and all of our hopes with you." Silvia talks softly. "That is all that two old people like us can want."

"What is it like in the United States of America?" I ask.

Enrique shrugs. "We only hear stories, but they say that everyone has toilets that make dung disappear. Everyone has water that comes out of pipes whenever they want. Even the poor have clothes, cars, and food. I think that the United States is a very good country, where rich people share their money and do not take away land from the poor."

"It is getting late," Silvia reminds Enrique.

"Yes, there is much to do," Enrique says. "Soon it will be dark. I need to nail boards over the top of the cayuco so water cannot enter in bad weather. Silvia will bring tortillas and fruit for your trip. We will also send bottles of water with you. If it does not rain, water will be harder to find than food. You will always have fish from the ocean if you can catch them."

"How can we help to get ready?"

"It is good if you sleep more. After you leave here there will never be good sleep again until you reach the United States of America."

I nod. I know this man and woman are very poor because of the way they dress. Helping Angelina and me will take food from their mouths for the next month, and so I say, "Thank you. Thank you very much. Someday I will try to pay you back." I hear my voice, and my words seem very small.

"You will pay us back by sailing to the United States of America," Silvia says. "If you can make it, you will keep alive our dreams and the dreams of all indígenos."

8

MY LITTLE SQUIRREL

I TRY TO SLEEP, but now my mind holds too many thoughts. From my pocket I take the compass that Uncle Ramos gave to me. This is the first time that I have looked closely at it. It is small but heavy. I lift the brass cover and touch the scratched and worn glass. When Uncle Ramos taught me how to use this compass, I did not know that it might save my life.

As I stare at the compass in my hand, I wonder if I am being very brave or very foolish. I do not know. I know only that I have much hope, but hope does not always tell the truth. Angelina is asleep on the bed, and I stare at her. I must not let her be hurt. She is young and innocent and does not understand that we are going on a very long and dangerous trip.

But Angelina is part of the reason that I must make this trip. She is a young indígena girl. Here in Guatemala, girls are not treated so well, and the indígena girls are treated even worse. This trip is something I must do for both of us if we are to ever know hope.

I close the compass and put it in my pocket again, then I look around the small room for anything that I can use. I am sure Uncle Ramos would want me to take what I need now. The only food I find is a small bag of rice and another bag of dried beans. I think these can be soaked in water to eat. I set these on the table. I find other things I can use: three empty water bottles, a fish line and a hook wrapped around a piece of wood. I find also the small and wrinkled map Uncle Ramos showed me the day we sailed his cayuco. I wrap the map carefully in a plastic bag. The map and the compass will be very important.

I put everything I have found into a plastic pail that is used to carry water. Now it is dark outside. I am glad there is only a small moon. This is a night I do not want to be seen. I wait for Enrique and Silvia. Maybe they have decided not to help us. Then footsteps come to the door again, and I hear a quiet "Hello." A big breath leaves my chest.

"Are you ready?" Enrique whispers, opening the door. Behind him Silvia waits patiently.

"Yes," I whisper. I go to the bed and lift Angelina into my arms. She still sleeps, so I carry her with one arm and pick up the plastic pail with the other. "These are things I can use," I whisper. "The water bottles need to be filled."

Quickly Silvia disappears into the dark with the water bottles. They are filled when she returns. "We have given you all the food we have," she says. "I am sorry there is not more. There is some fruit and dried fish, and I have made tortillas for you."

"I have gathered many coconuts for you," Enrique adds. "They will make food and drink, and the weight will be good in big waves. I have also nailed boards over much of the cayuco to keep out water. Now I think everything is ready." Enrique holds up a petate. "Maybe you can use this. Also I put some sugar cane under the deck. Chewing the cane will help you forget when you are hungry."

With no more speaking, we follow Enrique along the fence and down the same trail that I used the night I pretended to sail the cayuco. Tonight I am not pretending. Everything that happens now is too real, and I want to hide and cry. Tonight I must be strong, I tell myself.

When we reach the cayuco, Enrique takes the extra water bottles and pail of supplies I have carried. He pushes them with the other food into the small space under the deck boards on top of the coconuts. "You will have a hard time reaching these things," Enrique says. "Angelina will have to crawl under for you."

Angelina is awake now in my arms and looks around with big eyes that are heavy with sleep. "Angelina can be my Little Squirrel and get things for me," I say. "Do you want to be my Little Squirrel?" I ask her.

She nods. "Squirrel," she says, still yawning. "Is this a game?"

"Yes, it is a game," I say.

Silvia comes to my side and hands me a plastic bag that is smaller than my fist. "This is for Angelina when she cries," she says quietly.

"What is it?" I ask.

Silvia smiles. "Candy. When things do not go well, you can have some, too."

I do not know what to tell these old people who give us so much. The last time I tried, my words seemed small, so I hug each of them the way I once hugged my parents.

"We must go," Enrique says.

When we crawl into the cayuco, there is very little space. With boards nailed across the top, only one person can sit in the open back. Anybody else must lie underneath the deck or sit on top. There is room for only Angelina underneath, so I spread the petate on top of the coconuts for her to lie on.

Enrique stretches out on top of the deck. He points to the back. "You are the sailor now," he says. "I am only a passenger."

As I step into the cayuco, I realize how foolish I am. I am not a sailor. I am a poor indígeno who is afraid to push away from the shore. "Maybe this is foolish," I say.

Enrique pretends I have not spoken and pushes us

away from the dock. He hands me the paddle. "Move us away from shore before you raise the sail."

Carefully, as if I might break something, I dip the paddle into the water and take the first stroke toward the United States of America. And then I take the next stroke, and then the next. This long journey has begun.

"There is a good breeze from the west tonight," says Enrique. "That is good. You must sail out of the Río Dulce to open ocean before the sun comes up."

When I am away from the shore, I do what I have done many times in my dreams. I crawl forward over the deck and untie the pieces of rope that keep the sail bundled around the sail poles. Then I untie the lifting rope from the mast and pull up the sail and top pole. When the triangle sail cannot be lifted any more, I wrap the rope around a handle Uncle Ramos has bolted to the bottom of the mast.

The wind flaps the sail as I crawl past Enrique to the back. I lower the sideboard, then let the bottom sail pole swing farther and farther to the side until the wind suddenly fills the cloth. The cayuco tips but moves forward.

Enrique points. "Use your paddle as a rudder and face that direction." He points to faint lights in the distance. I look into the small darkened space below deck. "How are you?" I ask Angelina.

She pokes her little head out and asks, "Where are we?"

"We are on Lake Izabal, and we are sailing to the

United States of America."

She shrugs her little shoulders. "I knew that," she says, and crawls back into the darkness.

Enrique smiles. "I am not a real sailor, but Ramos has taken me sailing many times. Always he calls me his Second Sail because I help him. I think Angelina is your Second Sail."

I nod.

"You must practice before we reach the ocean. Change your direction and go that way," Enrique says. He points again.

I have to think, but I pull the sail pole toward me, then use the paddle as my rudder to hold the new direction.

"Very good," Enrique says. "Now go that direction." He points across the deck to the north.

This time I have to steer hard to the left and let the sail swing across the deck. When it swings, I must duck low or the pole will hit my head. I try to let the sail fill with air slowly so it does not grab the cayuco and tip it over.

Again Enrique nods. "I think you have sailed many times."

"I have sailed only once with Uncle Ramos, but I have sailed a thousand times in my dreams."

Enrique moves his body to face me. "Now we must talk about very important things. There are many things you must know if you do not want to die on this journey.

Do you understand?"

"I think so," I say.

"Okay. First, if the wind makes the waves big, you must paddle straight against the waves or sail with the waves. If a big wave catches a cayuco from the side, it will tip you this fast." Enrique snaps a finger.

I nod.

"This is the middle of May. It is a good time to sail north. You will have the currents always pushing you from behind, and you will also have the wind at your back pushing you most of the time. I think many mornings will be calm with clear skies, but in the afternoon as the heat grows, storms will come. These can be very bad. Be careful and always be ready for them. If you must take the sail down, take it down early. Lowering a sail on a narrow cayuco in a storm is very dangerous.

"The hurricane season is not supposed to begin for another month, so maybe you will be okay. But remember, nature does not always follow rules. Any week of the year there have been storms that sink boats much larger than what you are sailing."

Enrique points to his head. "Your head is what will keep you alive, not the boat. Remember that."

All the things that Enrique tells me are like rain on a dry field. I listen and try to remember every word. I ask questions about anything I do not understand. As Enrique talks, I stretch my feet under the deck. Angelina tickles the bottom of my foot. This is a game we have played many times, but tonight I cannot tickle her back because I must listen to what Enrique says. I wiggle my toes and hear her giggle.

"Before it is needed, you must practice lowering the sail," Enrique tells me. "When a storm comes, that is not a good time to do anything for the first time."

"What do I do at night?" I ask.

"If there is a bad storm, or if you get too tired, find protection if you can. There are empty islands and shallow reefs with mangrove patches. If it is hard for you to see the shore, then nobody on land can see you. That you must remember. Also if you sail inside the reef, you will lose the strong current that pushes you north."

"And what if I cannot find an island?"

"There will be those times. Then you must learn to sleep sitting up. The hardest time will be once you leave land at the north end of the Yucatán. Then you will sail day and night for almost two weeks. Your uncle Ramos talked to me of this journey many times. It was his dream. There will be little rest. You will find sleep in moments, not in hours. Be very careful when you are tired. Many sailors with big boats fear crossing the Gulf." Enrique smiles. "But this is also a very good time of year to be foolish. With luck the weather will be kind to you."

Angelina stops playing with my toes, and I think that maybe she has fallen asleep. I look out across the lake. It is hard at night to know where we are. All the lights seem far away and look the same. Alone, in the middle of this lake, I feel very small. What will it feel like on the ocean?

In the dark I cannot see Enrique's face. I see only the shape of his body against the sky. He has a proud chin and a big chest like a bull. I know he is an old man, but listening to him in the dark, I hear the excitement of someone whose heart this night is much younger.

"I wish I could make this trip with you," Enrique says after we have talked for a long time.

"I wish you could, also," I say.

"If a storm gets bad, keep Angelina close to you," he says. "If the boat tips over and she is caught under the deck, she will drown."

"Okay," I say, staring at the lights that grow brighter on the shore ahead. I did not know this trip would be this hard.

Enrique points into the dark. "We are passing the Island of the Birds," he says. "Soon we will pass under the bridge at Fronteras."

I look at the bright lights ahead. So much has happened so fast. Only last night I arrived in Fronteras in the truck of maíz. Last night Angelina and I sat in horse dung, afraid we might die with a drunk man in a pickup. And only last night all the people I knew and loved were killed. Even now I blink back tears. Yes, life is able to change very fast.

As we sail under the big bridge at Fronteras, Enrique becomes quiet. I watch the lights of the cars and trucks pass above us and then behind us. When Enrique does not speak again for a long time, I ask him, "Is something wrong?"

"We are on Lake El Golfete now," he says. "The fishermen say that there is a military boat guarding the entrance to the Río Dulce. This might be a very big problem."

"Why did you not tell me this before?" I ask.

Enrique smiles again. "Because you already have too many problems. This is the real reason I have come with you tonight. To try and help you get past the military boat."

9

WHITE BUTTERFLY

WHEN THE LIGHTS of Fronteras disappear behind us and we enter the water of the smaller lake, El Golfete, I feel a change. The wind blows stronger now. The waves splash against the front of the cayuco.

Enrique points. "We will stay along the north shore. If the winds blow strong, the middle can be very dangerous."

Enrique's words worry me. If a small lake can be dangerous, how will the ocean be? I use the rope to pull the sail pole in closer to the cayuco and use the paddle to turn the front toward the shore.

Enrique looks into the dark. It is as if he knows my thoughts. "On the ocean one meter waves will not be a problem," he says, "because they are far apart, and the cayuco can float up and down as they pass. El Golfete is a shallow lake and the waves are close together. A boat does not have time to lift back up from one wave before it hits the next. This makes El Golfete very dangerous.

"That is Cayo Largo," Enrique says, pointing to the dim shadow of an island in the night. Later he points again. "There is Cayo Julio." Now the wind changes direction and we follow the shore. The cayuco has slowed. I swing the sail to the other side and steer the front toward the open water. We move faster. Enrique nods his agreement. When I can see his face in the light of the moon, he looks worried. He keeps looking ahead and searching the shore.

I know now this trip from Lake Izabal could not be possible without Enrique. In the dark night everything looks the same. Between the clouds I see the North Star. But until we reach the open Gulf, the star does not help me. Even the compass would not help me if I could see it, because the shoreline is a dim shadow in the night that changes directions like a mountain trail.

Enrique speaks suddenly. "Now we must go to that shore." He points across the lake. "It will be darker there. When we reach the shore, we will take the sail down and paddle close to the trees. It will take longer," he says, "but if the military ship guards the mouth of the Río Dulce, this is the only way we might escape."

Soon I have changed directions, but crossing the lake is very hard. When the waves come straight from behind or from the front, the cayuco rides flat. Now the waves come from the side and make the cayuco want to twist and tip over. I push hard on the paddle to hold my direction.

Enrique stares into the dark. "This is the only way," he says.

Angelina is awake, and she crawls out from under the deck. Quietly she sits on the floor in front of my knees. I hear her breaths catch and see that she is crying, but I cannot take the paddle from the water now and hold her. Even now the cayuco tips very far to the side. Enrique lies almost flat on the deck to keep his weight low.

"If we tip over," Enrique says, "grab Angelina and hold on to the cayuco. It will not sink."

I nod. The cayuco does not want to obey me, and I struggle with the paddle. These waves are not good. The rough wood on the paddle makes my hands burn as I fight to keep from tipping or changing direction. I try to ignore Angelina's crying. It is a lonely and hurt sound.

"This is practice you need before being alone on the ocean," Enrique says.

"How much farther to the shore?" I ask.

Enrique shakes his head. "We will reach the shore when we reach the shore. Thinking about time only makes time pass more slowly. Remember that."

And Enrique is right. A thousand times my thoughts ask when this crossing will end. But the sky does not listen to me, and my questions do not make the cayuco sail any faster. My mind is numb before the shore finally appears like a dark shape out of the night. Tonight the sailing cayuco is not a butterfly gliding over the water. It is an angry cow being led through mud.

"Pull the sail down," Enrique tells me, his voice now only a loud whisper. "You rest. I will paddle until we reach the Río Dulce. Now we must be very quiet."

I do not argue. My arms feel like dead branches hanging from my shoulders. I keep my body low as I crawl to the front of the boat and untie the rope holding the sail up. Carefully I let the sail drop. My fingers are weak and blistered as I tie the sail and the sail poles together.

Angelina begins to cry louder.

Enrique speaks roughly. "She cannot cry now. Cover her mouth if she will not stop."

I know Angelina needs to stop crying, but I also know she will cry more if she is scared. I take her arm and say quietly, "Angelina, come sit with me. We will play a game. Help me look for butterflies."

Her crying stops with deep breaths that are like hiccups.

"Yes, butterflies," I say. "Come help me look. Quickly."

Angelina climbs onto the deck with me. "Where are the butterflies?" she asks.

I shrug. "I do not know, that is why you must help me look." I hold Angelina close to me on my lap and whisper, "We must be very, very quiet or the butterflies will be scared to come near, okay?"

Angelina nods and stares into the night.

Behind me Enrique begins to paddle. "There are small islands along this shore that will help to hide us," he whispers. He paddles so carefully that not a sound enters the night.

"Keep looking for butterflies," I whisper to Angelina.

She nods. "I think I see one," she whispers back.

"Where?" I ask.

She points her fat little finger at the black night. "There," she says. "See, it is black."

"I see it," I say.

Soon Angelina points again. "There is another black butterfly."

"Don't talk anymore," I whisper to Angelina. "It scares the butterflies."

Enrique paddles close to shore, each stroke strong and with purpose. Tree branches from the thick forest hang low out over the water like arms trying to grab us. We all stare hard into the black night. Enrique and I look for the military boat. Angelina looks for butterflies.

A loud splash under the trees scares me.

"It is only an alligator surprised by our passing," Enrique whispers.

Angelina rests her head against my shoulder and soon she falls asleep. Enrique stops paddling, and I look back at him. He has a finger to his lips and is pointing out at the water. I search the water but see only black. Still Enrique points.

Then I see the boat, dim, still, like a big bus waiting in the night. It is the military boat. I think I see flickers of light. Maybe it is a soldier lighting a cigarette. Maybe it is only the moon shining from a wave.

Enrique paddles again, moving even closer to shore. Every movement now is slow and takes great thought. I feel like a worm that crawls past a sleeping lizard. I hold my breath. The cayuco slows, then without warning, a branch breaks above us and falls into the water with a loud splash.

Enrique grunts his surprise as a bright searchlight comes to life on the military boat. I look up and see our mast has broken a low branch of a dead tree. The searchlight sweeps across the water and finds the shore ahead of us. Enrique paddles hard now, trying to move us sideways and hide us under the hanging branches. Still holding Angelina with one arm, I grab at branches and vines to help pull us into hiding.

The bright beam of light sweeps over us and searches the shore behind us. Angelina is awake again, and I have my hand gently across her mouth, ready to stop any sound she might make. She stares out from the hanging branches toward the bright searchlight with big eyes.

Again the white light flashes across our hiding place. It stops but does not find us, then it pokes into the trees behind us. Enrique and I hold our breath. The hanging branches hide us well, but I look up and see our mast above the branches. I hope the soldiers think that our mast looks like a dead tree.

Then the bright white light is turned off. We wait to see if the light will come on again. After we have waited a long time, I hear a deep breath come from Enrique's lips and a small hand taps my shoulder. Angelina pulls my head down so she can whisper in my ear. "I think I saw a big white butterfly," she says.

10

THE LAST BUTTERFLY

ENRIQUE DRIFTS the cayuco out from under the branches and paddles ahead like a ghost along the shore. All of the world seems to stop, even the wind, until the military boat disappears into the darkness behind us. Finally we can pull up the sail again. Enrique crawls back on top of the deck, and again I sit in the back with the paddle. Angelina wants to be near me, so I let her sit between my legs.

For the next half hour we do not speak because still we are scared of the military boat. We stay in the middle of the river where the current and the breeze are stronger. Also we do not want to be seen. There are many small homes along the shore.

The homes are dark now, and the people sleep. But during the day, I know this place is like my own village of Dos Vías before the soldiers came in the night.

Cooking smoke lifts up through the trees with the sound of children playing. Always there is the echo of firewood being cut with machetes. Some days people gather to help put new reeds on a neighbor's roof. During harvest, trails are busy with men bending forward against their head straps, bringing heavy loads of maíz on their backs down to their homes. The women grind the maíz in the village or they line the shore, washing clothes, rubbing and beating them against flat rocks.

As the cayuco moves closer to the canyon, the Río Dulce becomes narrow, and soon we can see both shores in the moonlight. Because the river bends and turns, the wind always changes. I cannot sail very long without pulling the sail closer to the boat or letting it out. Sometimes the wind disappears and I paddle. The night is not quiet. I hear birds and crickets and splashing fish. The sharp calls and humming of the frogs make the night seem alive.

Enrique whispers to me, "You do not have passports or immigration papers. That means you will be leaving Guatemala illegally. In every country you pass, you will be illegal. That is why you must not go to any shore until you reach the United States, unless it is to save your life. In the United States of America, maybe they will let you stay because you are children and your family has been killed. That is something you must hope for. That is your only hope."

Ahead of the cayuco, the shore becomes steep and

the wind blows harder as we enter a gorge. Soon cliffs lift high on each side of us and hide the moonlight. It is so dark I cannot see the front of the boat. Enrique turns and stares forward into the night, watching. I narrow my eyes to see. I do not want to hit anything. It will be good when the current takes us out of the gorge.

For a long time, we sail slowly through the big canyon. Once we pass a small fire burning on the shore. The light lets me see down the river. Then all is dark again. Sometimes the light of the moon drops between the cliffs and lets me see. My eyes grow heavy. Between my legs, Angelina sleeps, and I wish life could give me a moment of her sleep.

"Soon we will be out of the canyon," Enrique whispers. "Then it is not far to the old Spanish fort where I must leave you."

"Why is there a fort?" I ask.

"It is something the Spanish made hundreds of years ago to protect the lakes from pirates. Now it is a museum. But remember, there are still pirates on the ocean that will take all you have and kill you if they can. That is another reason you must stay far away from the shore." Enrique thinks, then speaks again. "You do not have a gun to protect yourself, so you must hide Angelina and use your head if a military or a pirate boat comes near to you."

"What can I do?" I ask.

"Do not speak Spanish. Pretend you do not understand

them. You must smile and speak Kekchi. Pretend the day is good and nothing is wrong. They might give up if they think they cannot speak to you and that you have nothing for them to steal. They will think you are only a poor crazy campesino who is fishing very far from shore with an old cayuco."

I do not like the talk of pirates and military boats, and I do not like that Enrique must leave me soon. He makes it easy to be brave. I think when he steps from the cayuco, I will be very scared.

Soon we leave the canyon. Now there is enough light to see the shore, but clouds fill the sky and rain starts to fall. The river current is weaker here. Ahead there are lights along the shore. Beyond those lights, I see nothing but black night.

Enrique points. "That is the ocean. Sail far out before you begin your journey north. Even then, stay far from shore. And there . . ." He points to a large dark shape on the bank. "That is the Spanish fort, the Castillo de San Felipe de Lara. Take me there. That is where I will leave you."

Obediently I steer the cayuco toward the dark fort. Again the air has the smells of smoke and motors. This lets me know we are near people.

"When we reach shore, it will be very dangerous," Enrique whispers. "There will be no time to say good-bye, so I will say good-bye now. What you are doing is very brave. You will be in our prayers. I hope that your journey is safe. I hope also with all of my heart that you will arrive at a place where you can live without fear and tell the story of what happened in Dos Vías."

"I will try," I say. "Thank you. You have taken many risks to help us."

Enrique shrugs. "I am old. I do not have much life left to risk. But you are young. Be very careful, and do not trust anyone."

"I trusted you," I say.

Enrique smiles. "Do not use up all your luck." He looks up at the sky and then says, "I have taught you everything I know about this trip, but that will not be enough. Now the ocean will be your teacher. You must learn well from her. I think you can make it to the United States of America, because you have a heart that does not quit, and because you have a mind that always thinks. Yes, if the journey can be made, you will make it. *Buena suerte*," he says, wishing me good luck.

And those are the last words I hear from this kind and very brave old man. Pointing with his hand, he guides me toward the shore. Carefully I pull in the sail pole, and we glide without sound closer to the old Spanish fort. I know Enrique has done all he can for me, but I also know he has never sailed a cayuco to the United States of America. I wonder if we will live through all the lessons that the ocean waits to teach us.

The silence of the night is filled with many feelings as the small cayuco nears the old fort. The rain falls harder now. I want to say something to Enrique, but I do not know what. Maybe I only wish to hear his voice again.

We are very close to shore now. As I let the sail swing free to slow the cayuco, Angelina wakes up. Enrique reaches out and rubs her small head and smiles, then he crawls to the front of the boat.

Because it is raining, I point under the deck and whisper to Angelina, "Hide where it is dry."

Angelina is obedient and crawls under the deck. I paddle the last few meters until the cayuco scrapes on the ground.

Enrique jumps to the shore and pushes the front of the boat back into the water. In silence, he points one last time to the open ocean, waves to me, and then turns and walks into the night without looking back.

Suddenly I am alone.

I stare after Enrique for only a moment, then I paddle away from shore to where I can lift the sail. The rain falls very hard now and drips from my arms and face.

"I want to see," Angelina says. She tries to stick her head out into the rain.

"Okay," I say, "but be very quiet. There are many butterflies here."

Angelina stares around at all the lights. Rain drips off her hair and down her cheeks like tears. We are alone on the water, and the small sailing cayuco is brave as it pushes into the night past the bright lights and out onto open water. Our ocean journey has begun. At this moment I do not feel so brave. I am very alone and very scared.

"Do butterflies like rain?" Angelina asks.

"No," I say. "I think this is the last time we will see butterflies for a very, very long time."

11

FIRST NIGHT

ALONE.

That is how I feel, so alone that it hurts. Maybe it would be better to be dead with my family. For a short time, I sail into the night thinking this thought, but then I think, No, Santiago, you cannot be sad if you are going to be strong. And so I look ahead at the ocean.

It is night, and still the warm rain falls, but I know my journey begins well. The waves are not big, and out here on the ocean I am not so afraid of being lost or running into military ships. Wind comes from behind me and lets me sail with the waves.

I turn and look behind me at the lights to see if anybody has seen me. I am not the only one who does not sleep tonight. Even now, in the middle of the night, people walk along the shore. The sound of their laughing and talking floats over the water like crickets in the night. As the wind pushes me farther from shore, the voices become harder to hear. I feel safer now. If anyone has seen me, maybe they think I am only a fisherman going home in his cayuco after drinking too much in the city.

Behind me, the lights grow smaller. Soon they blink like fireflies on the shore. A new, strange force begins to lift and drop the cayuco gently, as if a big hand is under us. It is the waves, but these waves are big swells of water that pass under the boat like hills.

Angelina sits quietly on the bottom of the cayuco between my knees. "I am hungry," she says.

"Remember, you are my Little Squirrel," I tell her. "Can you find the bag with tortillas? I think it is on this side." I point under the deck to the left.

Angelina nods and crawls under the deck.

Because of the rain, water leaks through the deck boards and slowly fills the bottom of the cayuco. I reach under the seat and find the plastic bowl that is used to empty water. Below the deck, Angelina moves and bumps against the boat.

"Did you find the tortillas?" I call.

She crawls out from under the deck with empty hands. She shakes her head. "I think there are pigs in the cayuco," she says.

"No," I say, laughing. "There are not pigs in the cayuco. If you wait until morning, I will help you find the tortillas."

"Okay," she says, "but maybe there are pigs in the cayuco."

I am still laughing as I look behind me. The lights on the shore are only little specks like stars now. I dare not go any farther out from shore because clouds do not let me see the North Star, and I have no way to look at the compass in the dark. If the lights disappear, I will have only the wind and the waves to guide me, and they can change. Carefully, I let the sail swing wide so the wind and current can push me to the north. Now the waves grow bigger.

Maybe it is good that I cannot see the ocean the first hours of this trip. I think I would be even more scared. Waves taller than my head pass the cayuco. When the cayuco does not lift from a wave fast enough, the next wave splashes hard across the deck and showers water through the deck boards. Spray wets my face, and I taste salt. Tomorrow I must find a way to fill the gaps in the deck.

Angelina crawls under the deck to escape the wind and spray. "Go to sleep," I tell her, but I know the water and the waves will not let her rest. I dream of sleep as I empty more water from the cayuco with the bowl. Sometimes a wave turns us to the side, and I must use the paddle very fast to turn straight for the next wave. When I am not fast enough, we almost tip over.

I am so tired. My greatest enemy on this trip will not

be pirates or storms or finding food. It will be fighting sleep, I think. If sleep comes at the wrong time, it can kill us.

I do not know how long this night has lasted, but already my whole world is changing. Now my world is the cayuco and the water around me. It is not my village, my family, the killing, my escape, or Enrique. Those things have become only memories from a different life that I lived at another time. Now all that is important is the next wave, the next stroke of my paddle, the next breath, the next meal, the next sleep. And always there is Angelina.

Before morning, the rain stops and the waves become smaller. Uncle Ramos has shown me how to find the North Star by following the lip of the Big Dipper. Stars blink through broken clouds, but there are still too many clouds to find the North Star. Once I see the moon, and it is a thin tired eye that is open just enough to watch us.

Angelina begins to cry quietly, so I let her sit again on the floor, leaning against me. It is hard to steer this way, but it is harder to hear her cry.

The lights on the shore disappear, and I think maybe I have sailed too far from the land. But then I see the black sky to my right turning to gray with the coming of morning. I feel good that I have lived through the first night. I pick up my machete and make a single notch along the side of the cayuco. Already I know that time will be very hard to remember on the ocean, so I decide to make one notch each morning when the sun comes up.

In the mountains where I am from, mornings come slowly. Here on the ocean, the morning comes fast. Soon the sky glows red, and it is not because somebody has burned a village. The red becomes a burning gold, and soon the sun breaks above the ocean like a bush catching fire.

Something floats on the water ahead of us. The cayuco passes through a long patch of floating branches and palm leaves. Maybe they are from the last bad storm. I take the paddle and lift as many palm leaves onto the deck as I can reach. This palm is called *pamac*. I do not know how I will use it, but I think everything I find out here on the ocean can be used.

Because I know this is only our first morning on the ocean, it scares me to think of how many nights and days Angelina and I will face. Enrique is right: thinking about time will only make the hours pass slower.

I decide I will do something each day to make the next day in the cayuco better. If I do this, maybe I will live long enough to finish this trip. I know that during the night, much water washed across the deck and leaked through the deck boards. This, I decide, is what I will try to make better today. But first I must eat and feed Angelina because she is awake.

"My Little Squirrel," I say. "Do you want to find the tortillas now?"

She nods her tired head.

I look under the deck and see the blue plastic bag with the tortillas. "There," I say, pointing.

Angelina crawls obediently over the coconuts and soon brings the bag and places it in my hand. I open it and find that many of the tortillas are wet with salt water. Carefully I take the wet ones and lay them on the wood deck to dry. "These we must eat first because they will not last as long as the dry ones," I say. "No food must be wasted."

When Angelina tastes a salty, wet tortilla, she wrinkles her face and closes her eyes, then spits out what is in her mouth.

"No!" I say with anger. "If you want food, then eat what I give you. This is not your birthday when you can eat only what you want."

Angelina begins to cry. Still angry, I pick up a salty tortilla and take a big bite. I force myself to swallow. Now I know why my sister spit hers out, but I am too tired to play games with her. I can use the fish line to try and catch a fish, but I do not think she will eat a raw fish either. Soon she will know that this trip is not a game. I force myself to finish the tortilla. Still, I feel bad for how I have spoken to Angelina, so I say, "Do you want a coconut?"

Angelina keeps crying, so I reach under the deck and

grab a coconut. It takes many hard swings of the machete to cut the coconut open. Milk spills from inside, but I break off a small piece of white coconut from the shell and poke it into Angelina's mouth. She tries to spit it out, but I keep it in her mouth until she tastes it and begins to chew.

I know coconut is hard to swallow after it is chewed, so I let Angelina drink milk from the shell. This I know she likes. After chewing more coconut, she stops crying, but I know that coconut does not stay long in the stomach of a child.

"I have to go to the bathroom," Angelina tells me.

I try to steer the cayuco straight into the waves as I help her lean over the edge. When she finishes, there is no paper to clean her. I cannot let her use salt water to wash herself. The salt will make her skin very red. Next I think of the drinking water and decide this cannot be wasted. The palm leaves I pulled from the water are too rough and soaked with salt. I have only the clothes that I wear.

I tear a sleeve off my shirt, and let Angelina use this to clean herself. If it rains, I will try to wash the sleeve because I know we will have to use it many times on this trip.

As the cayuco lifts and drops with the waves, I try to fill the cracks between the deck boards with strips of palm stalk. Using my machete, I force the stalk into each crack. I can only reach the cracks behind the mast. The cracks in front of the mast will have to wait until the water is calmer.

The clouds and rain are gone now, and a big sun climbs into a clear sky. The air becomes hot. All of my life I have worked outside in the fields, and the hot sun does not hurt my skin. But this heat is different. As the sun climbs higher, the water around the cayuco becomes like a mirror and makes the sun burn from all sides. The bright reflection hurts my eyes.

Angelina is hungry, but she is even more lonely. "I want Mama," she cries. I try once more to feed her a salty tortilla, but she will not eat. I do not want to use up the fruit we have right away, but finally I let her eat a banana. We both drink water. Maybe tomorrow I will let Angelina feel how much hunger hurts if she does not eat what I give her.

I know I need to find something for her mind to think about. I look up at the hot sun and at the palm branches I pulled from the water. When an indígena girl is only four years old, already she knows how to make tortillas and how to weave. She carries firewood and water. I know Angelina can do many things.

"Can you make us big hats with these leaves?" I ask Angelina.

She picks up a palm leaf and looks at it in her little hands. She nods, and begins to work. Soon her crying stops. She is small enough to lie under the deck in the shade while she works. When she grows tired, she sleeps, and then works more.

Me, I cannot sleep or escape the burning sun. The thought of sailing another night without sleep scares me. But for sleep I will need an island or calm water. The ocean does not give me either, yet.

12

FIRST STORM

ON THE OCEAN there is much time. Also much work. As Angelina weaves the hats with her small fat fingers, her lips bunch together with thought. She does what I must do—I must stay busy. Always my mind must think. This will help time to pass more quickly, and it will help me to forget the reason that I am here.

When the sun is straight above me, I take another drink with Angelina and I pull the back of my shirt over my head to keep away the sun. This sun can kill. My mother has told me many times that the sun is the heart of the sky and the father of all people. I think when the sun is this hot, it is not a good father.

My mind tries to think how many days this trip will last so I do not use the food too fast. All I know is what Uncle Ramos has told me. Maybe twenty days is how long he thought this trip would last. I take out the map and stare at the shapes and colors, but I do not know exactly where I am. This is the first map I have used. I cannot read it well.

I do not give up. I place my finger on the map where Uncle Ramos has told me Guatemala is, and I let my finger move to the north like the cayuco. Very soon the color on the map changes. This must be Belize. And to the north of that, when the color changes again, that is the Yucatán of Mexico. These things I remember from Uncle Ramos. The blue color is ocean, and there is much blue between the top of the Yucatán and the United States of America. Also on the map, many small islands follow along the shore to the north. Tonight I must find one of these islands to sleep.

I see blood on the map. The blisters on my hands are bleeding from the rough wood of the paddle. I rip strips of cloth from the bottom of my shirt and wrap these strips tight around the handle where my hands will be. I think this will help.

The waves are not bad now, so I crawl across the deck toward the front. The cayuco rocks in one-meter waves as I force palm stalks into the cracks in front of the mast. When the boat rocks hard, I grab the mast. I must be very careful and not fall from the cayuco. If I fall, the sail is tied in place so the cayuco will sail away with Angelina. That is a very bad thought. Maybe next time I should tie a sail rope around my arm.

When I finish filling the cracks on the deck, I climb

back to my seat and try to rest. I think the ocean is like my mind and never rests. Always my mind is thinking.

Angelina weaves what looks like a bowl. She makes me try the bowl on my head often as she weaves. I know when she finishes the bowl of the hat, she will weave the wide shade next. I watch Angelina work. Every moment that she thinks about the hats is one moment she does not have to think about being hungry or afraid.

In the afternoon, when the sun drops low in the sky, clouds build above me. Soon winds blow and the waves grow bigger. I think this is the afternoon storm that Enrique has told me will come on many days. As rain begins to fall, I make sure the plastic bowl is ready to empty water from the cayuco.

Angelina crawls under the deck, but she keeps weaving. The small cayuco splashes into each wave and sprays water over the front. I work hard to keep the cayuco straight. Now I must decide if I want to lower the sail. I remember Enrique's warning. If I wait very long, it will be too late. I crawl onto the deck and untie the rope that holds up the top sail pole.

As the sail and pole fall, the cayuco turns sideways to the next wave. I jump to the back and fight hard to keep the cayuco from tipping over. Angelina falls backward and hits her head on the side of the boat. She begins to cry, but I cannot help her. I am still fighting to turn the cayuco.

The next wave hits, and the cayuco rolls far enough

to let water wash over the side. When it rolls upright again, I am able to turn. Now I dip water fast with the plastic bowl. Angelina cries harder. I think maybe I will bring the sail down even sooner next time.

Between waves, I tie the sail and poles together. The heat of the sun is gone now, and the rain falls harder. The wind makes the waves grow until they become white on top. I keep paddling. The brave little cayuco meets each new wave with the sail poles swinging and bumping against its mast. The ropes slap against the wrapped sail.

Again and again, waves hit the front and spray salty water high into the air. Sometimes when the spray hits me, it is like a fist beating my chest. The deck keeps out the water that washes over the cayuco, but much water comes into the open boat where I sit. This water I cannot stop with palm leaves.

Always between strokes, I empty water from the cayuco with the plastic bowl. I know I am scared because my fingers hold the paddle so tight that my hands grow numb. Maybe a person does not win against the ocean. Maybe all I can do is fight back and try to stay alive.

I remember this as the storm punishes the small cayuco. I work to help the cayuco fight back. Each wave teaches me something different. Some waves are small and they make me think that I am a good sailor. Some come at the cayuco like a rolling bus. The ocean has many moods. Yesterday it was like a little old lady sitting down to visit. But today the ocean is angry and wants to hurt me. It does not let me run away. So I must be strong.

When big waves come, I tell them, "No, you will not sink me. This is not something I will let you do." If the wave is very big, I scream loud and paddle harder. I must not show that I am afraid.

But I am afraid, and Angelina knows this. Her cries hold much fear. I cannot tell her not to be afraid when I am so scared that I cannot swallow. I am afraid of death each time a wave washes water over the deck and each time the spray slaps my face.

Angelina stares at me, fear burning in her eyes like fire. I am all that she has. I cannot let the ocean kill her and take her to another world. Not today. I bite my lip until I taste blood. I do not know what will happen tomorrow, but today our world is the ocean and the cayuco. Our world is the rain and the sun and the wind and the hunger. I must fight to stay in that world until we reach the United States of America. Again I pull hard on the paddle and face the next wave.

I am still fighting the waves when a small mangrove island appears, ahead and to my left. The island is far away, but I must try to reach it before dark. It is my only chance: I cannot stay awake another night. Even now, my arms do not want to lift the paddle.

As we angle across the waves, I tell Angelina, "Come and sit between my knees. I do not want you under the deck if we tip over."

Angelina obeys but she is crying, "I want Mama! I want Mama!"

I do not answer her because I cannot give her what she wants. The storm still blows as we struggle toward the small island. The cayuco tips far with each wave, but I do not stop. We must cross the waves this way to reach the island. The wind blows harder as if to stop me. I fight the waves so hard, I do not see the sun leave the sky. It goes down quickly, and soon it is dark. I keep fighting with each stroke toward the dark shape ahead.

I have almost reached the island when the storm decides to stop. The rain keeps falling, but the wind and waves give up trying to kill me. I do not know how long the storm has lasted. That is like asking me how many tears Angelina has cried. I know only that my body is very weak when at last the front of the cayuco bumps against the mangrove branches. I pull up the sideboard, and I paddle into the thick mangroves until we stop. Then I crawl forward over the deck to the front.

Angelina's cries have changed to hiccups. "I want Mama," she cries again and again.

"Do not stand," I tell her loudly.

I know this island is not made of land. These mangrove trees grow from under the water and sit on a reef. Still they will protect us from the waves and the wind so that we cannot sink or tip over. I hear birds flying in the branches around us. I pull on the branches to float the cayuco deeper into the mangroves.

I tie a rope around a big clump of branches to hold the cayuco. Now we will not drift away as we sleep. Then I climb into the back. The sleeping mat is wet, and water has made a puddle in the bottom under the coconuts. But this does not matter. We will sleep on the coconuts. "Come, Angelina," I say. I push my feet under the deck and slide my body in until the deck keeps the rain from falling on my face.

Angelina crawls in beside me. Tonight I do not need to tell her to lie down and go to sleep. She clings to my side. I hug her and then close my eyes. Coconuts poke our bodies like big fists, and then sleep swallows me.

13

PIGS IN THE *CAYUCO*

I SLEEP SO HARD, even dreams do not find me. I know that as I sleep, the cayuco rocks, the hard coconuts poke my back, and water drips on my face. But nothing wakes me. These feelings are part of my sleep.

Many hours later, sometime in the night, I wake up. I do not remember where I am. Then I remember that I am sleeping under the deck of a cayuco that is tied to mangroves somewhere on the ocean. There is heavy weight on my chest, and it is hard for me to move. I reach my hand to feel my chest.

It is Angelina.

She sleeps on my chest pressed between me and the deck. I cannot be angry that she does not want to sleep on hard coconuts. Carefully I move Angelina off my chest and pull myself to the back to sit up. Rain still falls, but during my sleep the waves have lost their strength.

The cayuco rocks gently. I am still tired, but now my tiredness is only that of a lazy person who does not want to get up in the night and sail a small cayuco again on a dark ocean.

I do not think this rain will stop soon, but I know what I must do. Now there is no hot sun. The waves are gentle and roll north, pushed by a light breeze that blows from the south. The current flows past the mangroves like a slow river. It is better to sail now when the water and air are calm. There will be many times when the wind and the waves become angry.

Every part of me is wet except my mouth. My mouth is as dry as cut maíz under the hot sun. I stretch, and my muscles burn. Maybe this new day will go better. I stand in the rain and go to the bathroom into the dark water. Before leaving, I drink water from a plastic bottle, then carefully press part of the sail flat and let rain flow along a crease into the water bottles. The bottles must be kept full because rain might not fall again for a long time.

There is plenty of water now, so I wash the salt from my arms and head and legs. I also wash away the dirt and smell of horse dung that has been with me since the night we escaped. I must do the same to Angelina when she wakes up. Already her skin is dry and sore.

When I finish washing, I empty water from the bottom of the cayuco and untie it. The boat is heavy and hard to move. The current tries to keep me in the mangroves. Pushing hard, I float the cayuco backward.

Before I paddle out onto the waves, I pull up the sail and drop the sideboard. Because of the clouds and rain, the North Star and the lights of shore cannot be seen. But always the current flows to the north. It is my invisible friend.

Soon the current pulls me away from the mangroves, and the sail swings wide to catch the wind. I pull the sail in and out until the cayuco sails straight with the waves, then I tie the rope. Quickly the mangroves disappear behind me into the black night. I sail to my right, away from the reef, because the current will be stronger in deeper water.

I look down and yawn hard. Angelina still tries to sleep on the coconuts, but her grunts and groans tell me she is not happy. When the sun comes up, my compass and map will help me to find the shore. Now I relax and let the ocean carry us into the night.

Sailing alone in the darkness allows new thoughts into my head. I do not know very much about the United States of America, but I am sure that the *Americanos* do not know that Angelina and I are in a small cayuco sailing each hour closer to their great country. What will they do when they find us? Will they be angry and tell us to leave? Rain wets my face as I think about this. We will not be able to answer this question for many days.

Water slaps against the cayuco, and the waves lift and drop me again and again and again. After many hours, the rhythm becomes a part of me and I do not notice it anymore. Now the sky grows light. Movement under the deck tells me that Angelina is awake.

"Come sit with me," I say. "It is raining, but it is a good rain. I think the wind and the waves will not be strong today."

"I am hungry," Angelina says.

"Bring the fruit and the tortillas, and we will eat," I say, pointing below the deck. "We must eat the salty tortillas first."

Angelina crawls under the deck, and I hear her moving around. "Did you find the food?" I call.

"Yes," she answers, but she does not return.

I wait until I think that maybe she has fallen asleep. "Angelina," I call. "Did you find the food?"

"Yes, I am coming," she calls back again.

Soon she crawls out from under the deck and hands me the package of salty tortillas and two bananas. She smiles with a smile that tells me she hides something. I take out two tortillas and hand her one.

"I am not hungry now," she says. She pushes my hand away.

"Do you want a banana?" I ask.

She will not look at me.

"Did you eat some of the other tortillas when you crawled under the deck?" I ask.

She shakes her head hard like a dog shaking water from its hair.

"Angelina," I say. "You must not lie to me. Did you eat something when you crawled under the deck?"

Again she shakes her head no.

"If there are tortillas missing from the other bag, I will be very mad," I tell her.

"Maybe someone else took them," she says.

"Angelina, there is nobody else on the cayuco," I say.

Angelina's face becomes very serious. "I think there are pigs in the cayuco."

I look at Angelina and I think. "Okay," I say. "If there are pigs in the cayuco, we must chase them away."

"How?" she asks.

I reach under the deck into the big plastic pail. I hold up the little bag of candy that Silvia gave to us. "This is candy," I say. I take out a red piece and hold it so Angelina can lick it. After she licks it, she reaches to grab it but I hold it away. "If there are pigs in the cayuco," I say, "we must throw away the candy. That is why they come."

Angelina stares at the candy and shakes her head slowly.

I pull my arm back as if I am ready to throw the candy into the ocean.

"No!" Angelina screams. "There are no pigs. I ate the tortillas."

"You?" I say, pretending I am surprised.

She nods her head, ashamed.

Making my face very serious, I look at Angelina. "We

must always eat the bad food first," I tell her.

"Why?" she asks.

"Because we are playing a very important game now."

Angelina's eyes open wide with excitement. "What is this game called?" she asks.

I speak as if telling a secret. "It is called Staying Alive."

14

RIVER OF GARBAGE

AS THE SUN COMES UP, I explain to Angelina the rules of our new game. "We must always eat the food that will go bad first," I say. "We cannot eat or drink more than we need because our food must last a very long time. And each day we must think how to make the next day better."

"And we cannot let there be pigs in the cayuco," Angelina adds.

I smile. "Yes, that is a good rule, too." I look into the small bag and count twenty pieces of candy. "If you obey the rules," I say, "you will win one piece of candy each night before you go to sleep. If you disobey, I will eat your candy that day."

Angelina agrees to our new game, but I know this game will not be fun. Already her skin is cracked and dried by the salt water. Her hair is matted and tangled.

Soon hunger and pain will keep her awake. To make sure there are no more pigs in the cayuco, I keep the candy in my pocket.

I make Angelina lie on the deck, and I wash her body with the rain that runs off the sail. She does not understand why this is so important. There are many things she does not understand. She does not know what waits for us still on this journey or that her stomach will be empty many times before we reach the United States of America.

"Do you think you can finish the hats before the sun shines again?" I ask.

Angelina looks up at the rain and then she looks at me with bright eyes. "Do I get more candy?" she asks.

"No," I say. "But I will tickle you and tell you a very good story."

As Angelina works on the hats, I eat two salty tortillas and one banana. Also I take my machete and cut another notch in the side of the cayuco. We have finished our second night on the ocean. This is good, but I do not know what I have learned. I have done nothing to make tomorrow better, and the rules of this new game are rules I must obey, too.

Even now, small waves splash water back into where I sit. I pick up the plastic bowl and empty more water from the cayuco. I do not know how I can keep water from coming into the open back of the boat. When bad waves wash over us, they will sink us.

I look at the sail and think about another problem. I know now that this cayuco can survive very strong winds, but once the wind blows strong, it is already too late to crawl forward over the deck to drop the sail. Maybe there is a way to drop the sail without leaving the back seat.

Yes, I think—there is a way. I have two ropes that reach out over the water to pull the sail pole in or to let the sail pole swing out. There is one rope on each side. One of these is very long. The extra rope from that side is tangled at my feet.

I untangle the rope and use my machete to cut off a piece three meters long. Carefully I crawl forward and tie this extra rope to the lifting rope that raises the sail. I watch the waves carefully as I untie the lifting rope from the mast. I loop the rope under the handle that is bolted to the bottom of the mast, then I crawl back to the seat. It is important to keep the extra rope tight as I tie it around the seat. Now the lifting rope reaches all the way back to where I sit.

With this extra rope added, I can untie the rope from the seat and let the weight of the sail bring itself down. After it is down, I can wrap the sail around the swinging pole and tie it for bad weather. I know it will be hard to find the tie ropes when the wind blows strong, so I tie them to the sail pole, ready.

As I rest, I take out the machete and chop open a coconut. Angelina drinks the milk because it is something she likes, then I chop the coconut into little pieces that can be chewed on while it rains.

That afternoon, we pass two other boats, but they are far away. One boat is a big ship, the other is a fishing boat that carries tourists. Angelina's fingers stay busy making the hats. She works a little on one and then a little on the other. She wears her own unfinished hat while she works on mine. I think my hat will be worn out before she is done because she puts it on my head so many times.

As I watch Angelina with lazy eyes, my body relaxes and my eyes close for short moments. One thought bothers me. If sleep is hard to find now, what will happen when we have to leave land and sail without islands from the upper Yucatán of Mexico all the way to the United States of America? In the open Gulf, the wind and the waves will try to kill me. I will have no islands that will let me sleep.

No, I do not feel like a sailor now. Maybe a real sailor would not sail a cayuco to the United States of America. That is something only a fool does. But I know that soon, when I leave the Yucatán and sail across the Gulf of Mexico, by then I will need to be a sailor or we will die.

I am fighting sleep when the sky grows dark with the coming of night. Still it rains. I look across the waves and up at the low clouds. There is a large island with sand on the shores to the west of me. How good it would be to sleep on ground under a tree tonight. But this weather is good for sailing. If I waste this night with sleep, maybe the ocean will know I am afraid or lazy. I feed Angelina an orange and a salty tortilla before I give her a piece of candy. Then I let the island pass by us.

I ask Angelina, "Should we sail all night and look for stars that fall from the sky?"

Angelina looks up into the rain with doubt in her eyes.

"If the clouds go away, we will sail toward the North Star and try to catch it," I say. "Go to sleep now. I will wake you up if I see the North Star."

Angelina nods and pulls the petate over the coconuts and curls up. Soon she sleeps. Me, I sit and think. There is nothing to see, and only the sounds of the cayuco and the waves to keep me awake. There is no way to know my direction. All that I can do is sail with the waves tonight. The darkness becomes a tunnel without any end. Inside this tunnel there are waves and rain and wind. Each moment passes like an hour.

Memories of my family make me hurt, but they help me to stay awake. I think of my mother and father. I think of my brothers, Arturo and Rolando, and of my sister, Anita. I can remember Arturo laughing, hanging by his knees from a tree branch. I remember Rolando, who we all called the Singer, always singing funny songs. And Anita, who was only two years older than Angelina, but acted like her second mother.

Tonight my family is so alive in my mind, but in life they are all dead.

Angelina cries in her sleep. "Mama, Mama," she calls. A large wave rocks the cayuco, and she wakes up. It is good that there is rain tonight. Angelina cannot see the tears on my wet face when she looks up at me. I smile at her and try to be strong. Never in my life has a night been this lonely.

The rain ends when it is still dark. A fresh breeze brushes the waves like a big hand, and I pull the sail in tighter. If the wind stays like this, I will have to angle toward shore or away from shore. I decide to sail toward shore. I do not want to sail too close, but it has been many hours since I have seen even one light from the land.

When Angelina wakes up, the clouds have left the dark sky, so I show her the North Star. She nods but stares across the water as if she sees nothing. Right now her tired mind has forgotten the game that we play. She crawls back under the deck. My head nods as I keep fighting against the sleep that wants to drown me.

Now the waves grow bigger. Each wave makes me work to keep the cayuco straight. When the morning sun brings the first light, I have the machete in my hand ready to chop a third notch in the side of the cayuco. I make this notch a little bigger because this night has been harder.

Angelina still sleeps as I look for shore with tired eyes. This is when I see the first garbage. From far away, I do not know what it is. It looks like a dark curving river on top of the water. When I sail closer, I find a river of floating garbage. Somehow the currents of the ocean have brought all these things together as if looking for someplace to leave them.

I sail into the river of garbage and change my sail so I will stay with the garbage longer. I do not know what I am looking for. There are floating balls from fishing nets, many plastic bottles and bags, chunks of wood, old signs, plastic shoes, and even a gas tank from a car.

Ahead, something blue floats high in the water. I almost let it float past because I am not very awake. But then I see that it is a big blue plastic barrel. One end is crushed. I look at the boat and again at the blue barrel, then I paddle hard. I am thinking that maybe I can use the plastic barrel.

Angelina wakes up and watches me pull the barrel in beside the cayuco.

"What are you doing?" she asks.

"I am fixing the cayuco so my Little Squirrel does not get wet."

Angelina looks proud that I am doing something special for her.

There is water inside the barrel, and I cannot lift it from the water. I grab my machete. It is not easy, but I swing hard until I have cut a large curved piece of plastic from the barrel. I take this piece of barrel and place it on the deck. I move it around until it sits like a windshield that protects me from the spray. Now I must find a way to tie it to the cayuco.

As I think, the cayuco keeps floating in the river of garbage. Much of the garbage is made from plastic. I pass a torn plastic backpack, candy wrappers, and even some old plastic chairs and tables. I look for more of the plastic balls that are used on fishing nets. At last I find one that has rope trailing behind it in the current.

"What are you doing now?" Angelina asks when she sees me cut the rope from the ball.

"I am still making something so my Little Squirrel does not get so wet."

Angelina giggles when I call her my Little Squirrel.

"Can you help me?" I ask.

She nods.

I set the piece of plastic barrel on the deck. "Okay, hold it right here," I say.

Angelina kneels in the cayuco and holds the curved plastic. I take the tip of my machete and dig a hole in the deck and one in the plastic. After I tie the plastic guard in place with a piece of rope, Angelina crawls under the deck to finish my hat. I work to carve more holes in the deck and the plastic guard.

The sun is high in the sky when Angelina finally places my hat on my head with a hard push. "There, it is finished. Do you like it?" she asks.

I feel how the hat keeps the sun off my shoulders and neck. "Yes," I say. "How do I look?"

Angelina giggles. "You look funny."

I reach out and tickle her. "And how will you look when yours is finished?" I ask.

"I will look beautiful," she says, wiggling and laughing on top of the coconuts until I stop tickling her.

As Angelina works to finish her own hat, I keep carving holes. I space the holes the length of my opened hand apart. It is hard to work with the machete and also steer the cayuco. "I am almost done," I tell Angelina.

She still does not understand what I am doing, but she is excited because she knows it is something important for her. She watches with big eyes as I take the plastic rope I have found and push it through all the holes. Soon the plastic guard is tied to the deck. I know that now I will have to crawl over the guard to raise the sail. I slap the piece of barrel and push on it with my arms. It does not move. What I have done is good, but the next storm will be the true test.

Around me the waves build for the afternoon storm. Quickly I pull the bag of candy from my pocket. I give one to Angelina and I eat one myself. "Look, Angelina," I say. "We have played our game very well today. Now I can lower the sail without crawling over the deck. If a wave washes across the boat, it does not come inside. And you have made very good hats."

"And today I did not let any pigs into the cayuco," Angelina tells me.

"No, you did not let pigs into the cayuco," I say, laughing.

15

PIRATES

IT IS THE MIDDLE of the afternoon when the storm begins to build. A faint shoreline appears to the west. Also there is an island two kilometers north and east of me as I will sail into this storm. I am tired, but I will be even more tired when I cross the Gulf of Mexico. There, the waves and winds will be much stronger. It is important for me to know if the cayuco is strong enough. Also I need to know if I am strong enough.

Angelina crawls under the deck and pulls both hats under with her. The ropes are ready to take the sail down. I am tired but I, too, am ready.

Soon the rain begins. The wind blows strong, kicking water off the tops of the waves. The piece of plastic barrel I have tied in place works. The spray hits the barrel guard and flows around the side into the ocean again. Always I must fight with the paddle to keep the cayuco straight. "Do not crawl very far under the deck," I tell Angelina. "You must be close to me if we tip over."

Today the waves are bigger than before. I leave the sail up as long as I can, but soon hard gusts of wind grab at the sail and tip the cayuco almost on its side. I reach quickly to undo the knot around the seat. The knot is wet and tight and will not pull loose. The next wave hits me and another gust of wind catches the sail and turns the cayuco sideways. I paddle with all my strength to get straight. Again I fight to loosen the knot. The knot is so tight that my fingers cannot pull it apart.

Now the wind makes a sound like a cat wanting to fight. I brace myself for the next wave and pull at the knot with both hands. A very big wave rolls toward me, throwing patches of foam into the wind. Rain blows sideways past me. I know this wave will tip the cayuco if I cannot lower the sail.

I grab the machete and swing the blade down hard on the seat. The rope breaks loose, and the sail crashes into the water. The cayuco tips and rocks. Quickly I pull at the heavy sail and the sail pole to bring them onto the deck. Now the big wave hits us. A wall of water lifts the cayuco like a strong hand. As we go up, the ocean comes over the front of the boat and explodes against the barrel. I am protected. The barrel guard I have made has saved my life.

When the cayuco reaches the top of the wave, I am scared that I will fall down the other side, but the wave passes behind us as we rush toward the next wave. I know I must always keep the cayuco straight. If we turn sideways, we will roll down a wave like a log rolling down a hill.

I fight hard to wrap the tie ropes around the cloth so the wind cannot blow the sail back into the water. It is easier this time because the tie ropes are already hanging from the sail pole. When they are tied, I paddle into the next wave.

This storm is strong and does not grow tired quickly. Even after the dark clouds pass behind me, the waves stay big and angry. But I know now that the cayuco can survive big waves. I also know I must tie the lifting rope with a knot that can be pulled loose when it is wet and tight. When the wind loses its anger, I scramble to the mast and pull up the sail. This time when I tie the rope to the seat, I leave a loop in the knot.

I think I am beginning to understand the ocean. It is not like a person who is always this way or that way. No, the ocean is always a stranger. One day it is kind and lazy, the next day maybe it is angry or cruel. The ocean does not care how it treats a young boy and his sister in a cayuco. This is something that I must remember.

The waves and the wind stay strong the rest of the afternoon, so I look for an island where we can spend the night. A big one appears ahead of me, and I pull in the sail until the nose of the cayuco aims toward a small shore on the west side.

When I sail close, there is no sign of anybody. Still I am careful. This is not a mangrove patch. The wind pushes me closer. Ahead of me now, there is a small inlet. This will better protect us from the wind and the waves, so I pull the sail down and paddle the last hundred meters through a narrow opening into a protected bay.

I paddle next to a sandy shore. There is a place where a fire has been started, but it does not look new. At both ends of the sandy beach, there are thick trees that hang out over the water. Yes, this will be a good place to stay. What luck it is to find such a place in the middle of the ocean.

But then I think again. What if somebody else does come here tonight? What will they do if they find two children from Guatemala sailing a cayuco? No, now is not a good time to be lazy or foolish. Instead, I paddle the cayuco under the trees at the end of the sand. This will hide us if anybody comes.

Angelina is excited to get out of the cayuco. Her feet have not touched land for three days and three nights. "Stay very near the trees," I warn her as the cayuco scrapes the sandy shore.

Angelina climbs forward over the deck. When she jumps into the shallow water, she falls down. I, too, almost fall over when I step into the cool water to wade to shore. Our bodies have become used to the rocking of the cayuco. Now the sandy shore feels like it is also tip-ping and turning.

"Look!" Angelina calls with a giggle. She looks up at the sky and falls over again in the sand.

I try looking straight up myself, but must look back down before I also fall. As Angelina plays this new game she has discovered, I turn and look at the sky. The sun is almost down, and I know that soon it will grow dark. I am glad. Even if the trees hide us well, still I am scared somebody will see us. Angelina runs in and out of the water, splashing her hands and laughing. She finds seashells on the shore and brings them to me. She screams, "Look, Santiago! Look!"

"Yes," I whisper. "They are very pretty." I put my finger to my mouth, and she remembers she must be quiet. I know shells are something she has never seen before.

When Angelina is tired from playing, I take out the fruit and tortillas. I give Angelina one tortilla and half of one orange. I eat two tortillas and eat the other half of the orange. We have some dried fish, but I will save that for when I need to be strong crossing the Gulf. Also we have carrots, but I save them because they do not grow old so fast. Soon I must try to catch fish.

Because I do not know when we must leave the island, I make sure the cayuco is ready before I take the petate and lay it on the sand. Behind the trees, Angelina goes to the bathroom. This is something she has done many times today. I think that maybe the coconut milk is giving her diarrhea.

I tell Angelina to come and lie down beside me. "I

will tell you a story," I say. "But you must close your eyes."

She is obedient and she closes her eyes.

"A long long time ago," I begin, "there was an island where children could fly—even little girls."

"An island like this one?" Angelina asks.

"Yes, like this one," I say. "And on this island, there lived a big lion who wanted to eat the children. So he told them they could not fly anymore because it was hard to catch them. The children all flew high into the sky and laughed at the lion. They teased the lion. 'We can fly if we want,' they said. 'What will you do, fly after us and catch us?'

"'No,' said the lion. 'I will wait here on the ground. Soon you will have to come back.'"

I look at Angelina, and already she is asleep. This is good, because I do not know what the children will do next in my story. I close my eyes and am asleep before more thoughts come to my head.

I do not know how long I have slept when a buzzing sound fills the air. At first I think it is a dream, but when I awake, there is a boat without lights coming through the narrow opening into the bay. The dark shape motors toward the beach in the dim moonlight. The sound of laughing and yelling and cursing comes over the water.

Now Angelina is awake, too. I put a finger to her mouth, and we watch from under the trees. The boat comes to the shore on the beach. Five or six men crawl from the boat. They speak Spanish, and I can hear some of their words. They say something about the gringo boat they have robbed.

I am very glad now we are under the trees. I reach for the machete that is beside me. As we watch, the men start a fire. They have bottles in their hands and are drinking. I hope they cannot see us. We are close enough to throw a stone at them. One man stumbles toward us in the dark, and I am ready to run with Angelina when the man stops and goes to the bathroom. Then he turns and stumbles back to the fire.

I want to run and jump into the cayuco and paddle as fast as I can from the bay, but I make myself wait. The men are drinking very much and are still dangerous. Soon they will be even more drunk and tired. When they fall asleep, that is when we will leave.

Angelina understands some Spanish, and she hears the men curse and say things that are very bad. They brag about all the boats they have robbed. Two of the men talk about killing people. Tonight I wish that I did not understand Spanish. These are some of the pirates that Enrique warned me about.

Our sleeping mat is on the sand, and as we wait quietly, I scratch my skin. Angelina scratches, too. The longer we lie there, the more we itch and scratch. Something is biting us in the dark, but there is nothing we can do but wait.

It is a long time before the pirates fall asleep around

the fire. By now Angelina and I scratch madly and our skin burns like fire. Finally I decide it is time. I hold a hand over Angelina's mouth and lead her down the beach. We wade into the water, and I lift her into the cayuco. Again I put a finger to my lips, and Angelina nods. I point, and she crawls under the deck.

I am very careful when I untie the cayuco and push it out from shore. I keep the machete in my hand as I crawl in. Every move is slow because the pirates can see us if they look. I hope they are all very drunk and asleep.

I paddle close to the trees and stay where it is dark. When I look back, the fire flickers on the shore. Angelina and I, we must get away from this island. I know that during the storm today, we survived because I built the barrel guard for the cayuco. Now, again, we are alive because I have been careful.

At last I paddle from the shore and away from the trees that hide us. We have almost left the bay when I hear somebody by the fire shout. Then there is more shouting, and I see men pointing and running around the fire toward the boat. They have seen us.

My breath catches. I have only two choices: we can go back to shore, or we can raise the sail and try to escape onto the dark ocean. I think the ocean is our only hope. If the pirates captured the cayuco on the island, they would soon find us. The island is not big enough to hide us for long.

Like a mad man, I paddle the cayuco out of the bay

into the wind. Angelina sticks her head out from under the deck. "What is happening?" she asks.

"Hide under the deck," I say, letting my voice sound angry. "Do not come out unless I tell you."

She disappears.

Now the pirates have crawled into their boat, and I hear the engine start. At the same time, I feel the breeze in my face. If I raise the sail, it will be easy to see us, but if I paddle, they will find us even more easily. Quickly I raise the sail as I hear the pirates' boat speed up. In the dark, I cannot see the boat, but I can hear the engine screaming toward us. I reach down and pick up the machete. I grip it hard.

Now the sound of the motor is very loud, and I know that soon the boat will come through the narrow opening from the bay behind us. The motor becomes so loud in the night that I think it will hit us. Then there is a loud crash. Branches break, and the night becomes silent. The pirates' boat has hit the shore while coming through the narrow opening from the bay.

I feel the waves lift and drop the cayuco again as the island disappears behind us into the black night like a big shadow. I cannot swallow because my mouth is so dry from fear. I know that luck has saved us. For this I am glad, but I know that luck is not a friend that should be trusted.

Angelina again pushes her head out from under the deck.

"How are you?" I ask.

"Are the men gone?" she asks.

"Yes, the men are gone," I say.

"Who were they?"

"Pirates," I say, whispering as if I am scared.

"Like in a very scary story?" she asks, whispering back.

"Yes, like in a very scary story."

16

TWO SHORES

I SAIL NOW into a very black night on a dark ocean filled with angry waves. The wind is loud, but the North Star hangs in the sky, waiting for us. It is good to look at something that is so far away from the ocean and the pirates and the cayuco.

I do not know what time it is. I see the moon, but I am not sure where the moon should be when it is early or when it is late.

Angelina is awake. "I itch," she tells me, scratching her skin.

"So do I." I reach down and pick up a coconut. I hit it with the machete until the shell cracks. "Here," I say to Angelina. "I will put coconut milk on your skin." As I rub the milk over Angelina's thin arms and legs, I feel her bones and dry skin. She has already lost much weight.

She looks up at me. "Will this help?"

"Oh, yes," I say, even if I do not believe that my words are true.

"Do you itch, too?" she asks.

I nod and rub coconut milk on my own skin. And maybe I did not lie. The coconut milk feels good. But my hands still shake from escaping the pirates.

Angelina keeps scratching at her bites.

"The coconut milk will only work if you do not scratch your skin," I tell her.

She nods and keeps scratching.

As we sail, the night is long once again, lasting until my arms grow tired and I fight to keep my eyes open. Always I must look into the darkness and be ready for the next wave. Above me, a thousand stars remind me that morning still waits over the horizon. I spit at the black waves. To answer me, the wind blows spray hard in my face.

I have discovered that the first sign of morning is not a light that I can see in the sky. It is when the stars grow dim and begin to disappear. That is what I finally see this night. As I wait for the sky to become light, I take the machete and I make another notch in the side of the cayuco. I have four notches now. Another night has let me live.

In the daylight, a second shore appears to my right. I blink hard because my mind is mixed up. I still travel north with the wind and the current. This I know. The cayuco has not turned. But there are two shores now. One is still the shore far to my left. The second is closer to my right. Both shores reach as far as I can see to the north and as far as I can see to the south.

I think at first that I am sailing into a big bay and that we should sail south again. But I am not sure of this. Suddenly fear makes me breathe faster. I pull out the map and stare at it with big eyes. Then I look up at the ocean. No, this is not a bay. To the north there is only open water. I move my finger north along the shore on the map and I try to think where I am. Halfway up the coast of Belize I see many islands, but I do not think that is where I am. The islands are smaller than this land and too far away from shore.

My finger stops at the north end of Belize where a long island drops for many kilometers south from Mexico. At the north end of the island, the map shows a narrow opening that escapes to open ocean. But where am I? If I am south of this opening, I still need to sail north more. If I have already missed the opening, sailing farther north will take me into a big inland bay that will trap me. That would be a very big and dangerous mistake.

I see more boats now and this scares me. Will a military boat see us and know we do not have papers? As I think, I turn the cayuco and sail toward the big island until the west shore behind me disappears. I am sure now that I am someplace very bad because there is no current.

Still I do not know what direction to sail. North? Or south?

Because the wind is from the south, I take a big chance and sail to the north. As I turn the cayuco, I look again at the map. I do not think I understand maps very well. Each time I look, my thinking changes. First I think I am right. Then I think maybe I am wrong. I know I cannot sail up to a big white tourist sailboat and say, "Hello. Please tell me, where is the United States of America?"

I sail all afternoon, looking for the narrow opening between the Belize island and Mexico. With little wind and no current, I do not sail fast. The hot sun makes me feel like an ant crawling across a desert. On the shore, there are only fishing camps. I pass small islands and bays, but still there is no place where the water opens to the ocean. Maybe I am not where I think I am. Maybe I am someplace the map does not show. Inside of me, fear pulls my stomach tight like a great knot.

I am looking so hard for the ocean, I do not see a big sailboat that catches up to me from behind. A loud horn blows, and I turn. I think my heart stops. The boat is close enough to hit me if it turns only a little. The boat has a great sail and a mast that is the size of a tall tree. Standing on the deck are many white people who wear swimsuits and sunglasses. They are waving. One takes pictures of my small cayuco with her camera. I do not know why these people look at us and take pictures.

Maybe they think Angelina and I look funny with our big hats. I keep my head down and tell Angelina to hide under the deck.

The sailboat does not slow. Soon it is far ahead of me. Still moving fast, it turns and sails east. I think it will hit the island, but it disappears beyond the island, still sailing east.

"Angelina," I say, letting my voice be loud. "Maybe we have found the ocean again."

Angelina crawls out from under the deck and looks around. "There is no wind and waves," she says.

"They wait for us out on the ocean with the current," I say.

"I do not like wind and waves," she says.

I smile. "Sometimes they are friends," I say. "They take us to the United States of America."

The small cayuco sails until I can see around the north end of the island. At first I want to cry because I see only land. The big sailboat is stopped in a bay. But then I see a fishing cayuco going behind the trees into what looks like a big river. I look at the bay and I look at my map. I do not see any big river on the map where I think I am. And I do not think a fishing cayuco goes to a river to fish.

I know what I do now is very dangerous, but I follow the other cayuco. There is no wind, so I let the sail drop. Soon I am paddling along a narrow channel of water that is very shallow and only thirty meters wide. Below the cayuco there is green seaweed and sand. Soon I see other small boats. Some have motors and pass by me. I keep paddling and do not look up at them.

I am almost ready to give up and turn around when the channel bends. Ahead of me, water reaches all the way to where it meets the sky. Happiness explodes inside me. It is ocean as far as I can see. I paddle faster. Angelina knows that something makes me very happy, and she claps her hands.

Much more time passes before I have paddled through the opening and the cayuco lifts and drops with the ocean swells again. When the winds pick up, I raise the sail. Again the current comes with an invisible hand and pushes us to the north. I realize that I have changed in only four days. When I first sailed from the Río Dulce, winds and waves scared me. Now I am happy to find them again. I only hope they do not become angry with me.

I know now that the land to my left is Mexico, so I sail east until the shore is once again only a thread resting on the water. The spray of salt water wets my skin, and the cayuco pushes through the waves. The other fishing boats do not come this far away from shore. Once more I sail alone.

Soon it will be night, and we have not eaten all day. Still I am happy to be back on the ocean. We did not escape trouble today with thinking or with bravery. Today luck rode with us again in the cayuco. I do not like this because maybe next time luck will not be so kind.

"Are you hungry?" I ask Angelina.

She nods. "I want something different."

"We have dry beans," I say. "But we cannot cook them. Maybe we can soak them in water before we eat them. Do you like beans?" I ask.

Angelina shakes her head. "I want hot chicken."

"Okay," I say. "Go catch the chicken, and I will start the fire."

"You cannot start a fire in the cayuco," she says.

"And you cannot catch a chicken on the ocean," I answer. "We will eat tortillas and fruit again tonight, but we will soak beans in water for tomorrow. They will be hard, but I think it is something we can eat."

With an angry face, Angelina brings the tortillas. "Tomorrow I will look for chickens," she says.

I smile. "Okay."

Tonight, for the first time, we eat tortillas that are not salty. Angelina likes this, but tonight she does not smile. I think all four-year-old children have nights when they do not smile. When we finish, I cut a papaya in half and we eat all of it because it will be soft by tomorrow.

Angelina finishes before me and quietly brings the bag of beans from under the deck. To help her, I take a bottle of water that is half empty and pour dried beans through the top. In the morning we will see how beans taste when they are not cooked and can only be soaked in water. I think that tomorrow will be a good day to begin fishing, too. Raw fish does not seem so bad now.

After Angelina falls asleep under the deck, I begin the next long night. Tonight, as I stare at the waves, the water passing beside the cayuco glows green like a dim candle. The glow dances and flashes. I do not know why this happens, but tonight I do not care because my mind is numb.

Since the night of the killing, my mind has asked many questions. How do I escape the soldiers? How do I find the home of Uncle Ramos? How do I sail a cayuco? What do I eat? How can I live in a storm? Will the pirates see me? How do I take care of my little sister? And what if I am lost? These are only some of the questions that my mind has needed to ask. This is why my mind has grown more tired than my body.

Tonight my mind does not care where I am or where I go. I do not care if there are more soldiers ahead or if there is not food to eat. Tonight my mind is too tired to worry. I think only of sailing the cayuco.

I stare up at a sky filled with stars. After I stare a long time, I see one star fall into the ocean. It is so bright I think it will land in the cayuco. I think that this trip is only a dream that will end when I wake up.

17

I AM STUPID

MY MACHETE makes a loud sound when I cut the fifth notch in the side of the cayuco. The sound wakes Angelina.

"I am hungry," she says, even before she rubs sleep from her eyes.

"I am, too," I say, but I know that we have only three tortillas left, and they have green mold. Still, we must eat them. I smile. "This morning we are lucky," I say. "We can eat tortillas and beans."

Without being told, Angelina brings the tortillas and beans. I push my machete into the top of the bottle and use the blade to lift beans from the water. I put some in my mouth and chew. The beans are not hard, but I cannot say they are soft. They are like a carrot or coconut. They can be chewed but are hard to swallow. Water helps.

126

Angelina watches me scrape mold from a tortilla. I fill the tortilla with beans and give it to her. She does not complain, but her face tells me she does not like what she eats. As she chews, she stares out across the ocean. Her eyes blink to hold back tears. I think maybe her little stomach hurts because she is so hungry. She stares the same way a stray dog stares when it eats garbage.

I also chew on a tortilla with beans and say to Angelina, "This will help us to win our game."

"Staying alive," Angelina says.

I nod. "When we win, we will be able to eat chicken and hot tamales. There will be fresh tortillas with lime and salt and garlic. We will even have soup made from lamb like when there is a wedding or a child is born in the village." When Angelina does not answer me, I say, "Angelina, today we will catch a fish."

Angelina stares across the waves as if she does not hear my words. She looks at me only when she needs more water to help her swallow the dry tortilla and beans.

"I do not like our game," she says suddenly. When I do not answer her, she asks, "Can I have coconut milk?"

I shake my head. "I think that is what gives you diarrhea."

As I eat, I look at the ocean and try to think about what I can do to make sailing tomorrow easier. I know I need to make a rudder with the paddle or I will never dare to sleep. Carefully I use the machete to cut a notch behind me in the back of the cayuco. I make the notch only big enough to hold the handle of the paddle. Now I can put the paddle in the notch and steer the boat without always lifting and pushing.

Already the sun climbs higher and brings more heat. Today the waves are like small rolling hills that follow the cayuco from behind. The wind lets me swing the sail wide. I put the paddle in the notch and lean against the handle to keep the cayuco straight.

I know I must find rest today, but I must also be able to wake up. "Angelina," I say. "I need sleep. I will sit in the seat, but today you must sit between my legs and be my eyes. Wake me up if you see other boats or big waves or if we start to turn. Okay?"

Angelina takes another drink of water and nods. She pulls on her hat then stands and pushes mine over my head. Quietly she sits on the floor between my feet.

I am very proud of Angelina. She is only four, but already she knows what she must do. I think maybe she knows that this is not really a game. I think there are many things Angelina knows but will not speak of.

Before I let myself sleep, I pull out the fishing line from the plastic pail under the deck. The line is wrapped around a small chunk of wood. There is only one hook on the line. I rip off a piece of dried fish and push it over the hook. I am not a fisherman, so I do not know what fish want to eat.

Carefully, I drop the hook into the water and unwrap

the line until the hook pulls under the water about ten meters behind the cayuco. I am too tired to hold the line, so I tie it around my waist. "Angelina," I say, "if a fish moves or pulls the line, wake me up."

Angelina nods.

With the paddle wedged in the notch, the cayuco sails straight. I look around me once more before I close my eyes and fall asleep. Soon the sleep of the dead captures me. I sleep until I relax and fall to the side. This jerks me awake from my heavy sleep.

I look down and find Angelina asleep also, her head resting on my legs. The cayuco still sails well, so I do not wake her. Little sisters do not make very good sailors or fishermen. I turn and find that the fishing line still pulls straight behind us. Again I fall asleep.

I am sleeping hard when a little hand wakes me. It is Angelina jerking on my ear. "Fish," she says. "Look at all the fish."

I wake up fast because I think we have caught something.

Again Angelina says, "Look, fish!"

What Angelina sees is many dolphins swimming around the cayuco. Their backs roll above the water, and they look like they are playing. Sometimes they jump high out of the water. One comes up very close beside the cayuco. Angelina reaches out and tries to touch it.

"Why are the fish here?" Angelina asks.

"These are dolphins," I say. "They are not fish. Uncle

Ramos has told me they breathe air and play like dogs."

"Why do they jump beside the cayuco?" she asks.

"Because they know we are on a very long trip and they feel sorry for us. They know we feel lonely and they want us to laugh. See how they smile?"

Angelina nods. When she turns to look at me, she is smiling. "The dolphins make me smile," she says.

As the dolphins play, I smell a bad smell. I do not have time to think about it because suddenly I feel a heavy pain in my stomach. It is like I have swallowed a coconut without breaking the shell. I need to go to the bathroom almost faster than I can pull my pants down. "Angelina," I say, "look at those dolphins." I point to the front of the cayuco.

When she looks forward, I pull my pants down. The cayuco has a flat back where I have made the notch for the paddle. I lean my bottom over the back. It is like a firecracker exploding inside of me, and Angelina turns to see what the noise is.

"Look at the dolphins," I say with an angry voice.

Angelina looks again to the front, but I hear her little voice giggle.

"What is so funny?" I ask.

"When you went to the bathroom, you made the same sound I made."

"Did you go to the bathroom when I was sleeping?" I ask.

She nods.

I am finished, so I reach under the seat and use the dirty sleeve from the shirt to clean myself. "Did you go into the water?" I ask.

She shakes her head. "I tried but I almost fell into the ocean. I went there." Angelina points under the deck at the bottom of the cayuco.

Now I know what the bad smell is. I am very angry. The bottom of the cayuco is not dry. Because there is water under the coconuts, now all the coconuts are dirty and will have to be washed before we can eat them. I want to be mad at Angelina because I am very tired, but I ask her in a patient voice, "Why did you not wake me to help you?"

"I kicked you, but you did not wake up."

"Did you clean yourself?" I ask.

She nods.

"How? The sleeve was behind me."

Angelina will not look at me.

"How?" I ask, my voice louder.

Angelina points her finger at the leg of my pant.

I look down. My pant leg is smeared with brown. I shake my head and hold my breath to keep back my anger, then I smile a tired smile. "I need more sleep," I say. But first I swing my leg into the ocean and wash the leg of my pants. "Next time, use your dress."

Angelina shakes her head. "I do not want a dirty dress," she says.

I point at the coconuts that are the most dirty. "Hand

me those and I will wash them."

Angelina shakes her head.

"If you do not hand them to me, I will clean them with your dress," I say. "The same way that you have used my pants."

Angelina crawls forward quickly and picks up the dirtiest coconut. She pinches her nose with one hand, and gives me the coconut with a stiff arm.

When I finish cleaning the coconuts, I take the bottle with the beans and tie it near the mast on top of the hot deck. Maybe sitting in the hot sun all day will make the beans better for our stomachs.

"If you have to go to the bathroom, you must wake me up," I say.

"I think I will hit you on the head with a coconut," she says.

I do not laugh because I know she will.

I look down now and find only a short piece of fishing line waving from my waist. The line is broken where it has rubbed over the back of the cayuco.

I am angry at myself. I know I have done something very stupid today. I had only one hook, and now it is gone. Did I think the cayuco would fish for me because I was tired? Big tears come to my eyes to tell me that I am stupid, very stupid. Maybe this one mistake will kill us.

Carefully I wrap up the broken fishing line. I blink my eyes to hold back the tears as my tired thoughts float above the waves with the wind. This is how I sail the rest of the day. I try to sleep, but thoughts keep me in a world that is someplace between awake and asleep. As long as I can see the faraway shore, I do not worry.

In this part of the ocean, there are only a few islands, but I know I sail close to a reef because once, during the afternoon, I look down into the clear water and see the bottom. Also the current has slowed.

As night comes to the sky, I sail near the floating balls from a fisherman's net. I do not think anyone can see me from shore, so I lower the sail and paddle beside one of the balls. What I do is very wrong, but maybe it is okay because I am only a young boy who has lost his only hook and is trying to feed his little sister.

The net is heavy, but I pull it up until I find a silver fish tangled by its head. The fish is still alive, so I hold it with my hand and chop the head off with my machete. The net drops back into the water with a loud splash. Quickly I raise the sail and keep sailing. I do not want someone to catch me.

As I sail, I cut the fish apart. Angelina does not wait. She reaches out and grabs a piece of meat before it is cut away from the fish.

"Wait," I say, smiling. I know her little stomach is very hungry. Five days ago, she would not eat a fresh tortilla wet with salt water. Now I must tell her to wait before she can eat a raw fish covered with blood.

18

NOTCH NUMBER SIX

I REMEMBER WELL the night when Angelina and I sailed from Guatemala with the moon small and the night dark with rain. Tonight the sky is filled with stars and the moon is bigger. The waves roll north and east to my right. If I am going to sleep during this night, I must sail with the waves. They will take me away from shore, but I know that tomorrow I will find the shore again. Land does not move.

I am not so afraid of being away from the shore now because I am learning more about the ocean. The winds and the waves east of the Yucatán are more kind to me than the waters near Belize. But I know this is something that can change, so I will not be foolish.

My hands and my backside are sore. Because the wooden seat is always wet with salt water, my skin is raw from sitting. Sometimes I kneel so I do not have to sit, but then my knees become red and sore. I even stand sometimes, but that is dangerous.

I worry about Angelina because her skin, too, is becoming very burned and cracked. Her skin is not thick and hard like mine, and she does not understand why it hurts. Sometimes big silent tears wet her cheeks because her backside is so sore from diarrhea. I do not know if she is sick or if the food or coconuts make her this way. When rain comes, I will wash her again.

Angelina is brave and does not cry very much now. She sits quietly under the deck. Sometimes she scratches at her dry skin. Sometimes she picks at her nose. I give her coconut and sugar cane to chew. This helps her to forget the hunger she feels.

Yes, Angelina is a brave girl, but I think her silence also tells me that something is wrong. She does not talk about Mother or Father, or about our brothers and sister. I know that she carries memories of them and of home and of the night the sky turned red. I reach out and give her a big hug the way Mother once hugged her. She pushes me away. She is a very sad girl.

I know that this trip is killing Angelina a little each day. That is why I must sail through the coming night. Also tonight I must sleep when I am sailing. This is dangerous, but if I do not sleep, maybe tomorrow I will fall asleep when the winds and the waves are even stronger.

And so I sail into another night. I sleep, but always I think a part of my mind stays awake. In the middle of the night the waves grow bigger and the wind grabs at the cayuco. I decide to sleep a little more. I will let the ocean keep pushing me north. Each minute I sail, I am a little closer to the United States of America. Soon I will lower the sail, I tell myself.

That is my last thought before I wake up falling sideways into the water. There is a big splash as the mast hits the water and a giant wave rolls over the cayuco from the side. Angelina screams and I know I must find her.

"Angelina!" I yell. "Angelina!"

I think she is still inside the cayuco, so I swim beside the boat and reach my arm under the deck. My fingers find her small arm, and I pull her to air. She coughs and spits, then screams like she is dying. I hold the cayuco with one hand, and with the other, I hold Angelina.

In the dark, the waves lift and drop us, and the wind is so strong, it makes me close my eyes. But we are okay. Something bumps my shoulder. I turn and find the paddle floating beside my head.

"Hold the cayuco," I shout to Angelina, pushing her near the seat. I grab the paddle.

With her little hands, Angelina holds on to the cayuco. I move fast. What I do now will save us or let us die. "Hold tight!" I shout again at Angelina as I push the paddle under the deck where it will not float away. Then I reach for the seat and pull loose the sail rope. I crawl up on the side of the cayuco. Somehow I must lift the mast from the water.

First I lean far over the side, but my weight is not enough. The sideboard is out of the water, so I crawl out on the sideboard as far as I can. This lifts the mast some from the water, but the wet sail is still too heavy.

Angelina screams louder.

"Hold on!" I keep shouting. I know I do not have very much time. I must lift the mast from the water.

As fast as I can move in the darkness, I crawl to the bottom of the mast. I pull the sail to the deck and tie it around the two sail poles. Next I grab the sail rope I have let loose. I pull it free of the mast and crawl back onto the sideboard. Now I can stand up and pull on the rope that comes from the top of the mast.

Angelina still screams and the wind gusts.

I lean back and pull with all my strength. For a moment, I do not think I can move the cayuco, but then the mast lifts slowly from the water. As it comes up, I crawl off the sideboard into the cayuco.

When the cayuco tips upright, it rolls fast, and I must jump into the water so that I am not hit by the sail pole that swings across the deck. The boat is filled with water, but it sits upright with Angelina floating inside, still holding tight to the side and screaming.

Another wave hits and almost tips us over again. I need to turn the front into the waves. I pull myself aboard and reach under the deck to find the paddle. My hand finds nothing. Another wave hits, and I lean almost into the water to keep the mast up. Again I reach under the deck. If I have lost the paddle, I cannot sail the cayuco. Still I feel nothing. I almost give up when my fingers touch the end of the handle. I hold my breath and go underwater and grab it.

With Angelina in front of me so she cannot fall out, I paddle until the front of the boat faces the next wave. Even filled with water, the sides of the cayuco are above water. The plastic bowl that we used to empty water is gone, so I scoop water out with my hands. "Help me," I tell Angelina. "This is part of our game." I do not think she can help very much, but it will make her less scared.

Angelina watches me, and then she splashes water from the cayuco with her hands.

I paddle to keep us straight, and then I scoop water with my hands. I paddle, then scoop water, paddle and scoop. For the next hour that is all I do. In the light of the moon, I see Angelina's face. Fear makes her eyes shine.

Maybe it is because I am so scared, or maybe it is because I am crazy, but I start to laugh. The wind tries to quiet my voice, but I shout, "Angelina, this is our game, and we will win!"

Angelina watches me. She does not know what to think. I keep laughing and paddling and scooping. When I look at Angelina again, her face has found a smile and she splashes at the water with her hands. "Win," she says. Her weak voice still shakes with fear. "We will win."

"Yes!" I shout. I tighten my hands into fists and I wave them at the sky. "We will not die!" I scream. "We will live and tell the world what has happened to our village!" Yelling like this keeps tears from my eyes.

I do not know what time it is. I think maybe when things like this happen, time goes away. All that is left is this moment and the next.

When much of the water is emptied from the cayuco, I make a cup with my hand and pull water up the side. Finally the sun comes up. Both of my hands bleed, but I raise the sail again. I know that tomorrow or maybe the next day, I will leave land and sail across the Gulf of Mexico. When that time comes, I must be more ready than last night or we will die.

I make up my mind. This thing that has happened, it is not bad. During the night, the cayuco did not break. Angelina is still alive and I still have a paddle. Now I know that I must make something for Angelina so she cannot drown. I will tie everything to the cayuco so I cannot lose it, and I will be ready for winds and waves that are even stronger than these.

I see the machete in the bottom of the cayuco. This is something else I cannot lose. I pick up the machete and make another big notch in the side of the cayuco. Now there are six notches.

"Look, Angelina," I say. I pick her up and set her on my lap. "Look at all these notches. Help me to count them." I put my finger out and touch each notch with my finger. "One . . . two . . . three . . . four . . . five . . . and six." I hug Angelina. "When there are twenty notches, I think then we will win our game and be in the United States of America."

Angelina looks up at me. She asks me, "If not, where will we be?"

I take a deep breath. "I do not know," I say.

19

ANGELINA'S DOLL

AS I SAIL NORTH, the shore sometimes disappears. I do not worry because I think the map shows big inlets along the Yucatán. Each day I think I sail the distance of three fingers up the map. If this is true, we will leave the Yucatán and begin crossing the Gulf of Mexico by tomorrow night.

I am very lucky I have not lost the map that is in the pocket of my shirt. Maybe next time, luck will not be so kind. The map is wet from being in the water, so I am careful when I unfold it from the plastic bag. I hold it on the hot deck to dry in the sun.

As the map dries, I stare at the shapes and try to learn every country, island, and inlet. To help me remember, I use the tip of my machete to scratch the shapes of each country into the wood deck. I trace Guatemala, Belize, the Yucatán, Cuba, and the state called Florida. I even carve the names of each in the deck. Now, when blowing wind makes it hard to look at the map, or if waves tip the cayuco and I lose the map in a storm, still I will have something I can follow. I do not want to always ask for luck.

I give Angelina a little piece of dried fish and a carrot to eat. I smell the beans. Maybe I will let them soak one more day. I eat one banana that is very black and soft. I also break open a coconut. My stomach hurts from being hungry, and chewing on coconut makes my stomach think it is eating. I save the sugarcane for Angelina because that is something she likes.

As we sail, I always look for the floating balls from a fisherman's net. If we can eat fish again like yesterday, I think we can stay strong. Now I am glad the waves are not big because there is much to do.

Angelina helps me pull out everything we have—except the coconuts—into the sun to dry. We have little food, only the fruit, some broken stalks of sugarcane, the wet bags of beans and rice, two dried fish, and the water bottles. I look at the other things I have. There is the compass, my machete, the pail, some fishing line with no hook, three short pieces of plastic rope, the paddle, and the candy. I pull the candy from my pocket. It is melted by the water into a hard ball no bigger than the compass.

The only thing lost during the night is the plastic bowl for emptying water and the sleeve we used to clean ourselves. I cut my shirt with the machete and tear off the other sleeve. Maybe tipping the cayuco last night has helped me. It makes me know I must be more ready when I cross the Gulf. Also the ocean water has washed away the bad smell under the deck.

With the extra plastic rope, I tie the machete and the paddle to the cayuco. It will be hard using them with small ropes tied to the deck, but I must not lose them. I have the wet bags of beans and rice hanging high on the mast to dry. The fruit I will eat only when it becomes very soft with age. I am worried that I do not have enough food to cross the Gulf. When food is wet, it does not last, and out on the ocean everything is soon wet.

When all of the food and supplies are stored back under the deck, I take the last piece of the plastic rope left from the river of garbage, and I tie it around Angelina's chest. To this loop of rope, I tie two empty water bottles. Now Angelina can pull the loop around her chest when the weather is bad. I will make her sleep with the bottles at night, too. The empty bottles will float and keep her alive if the cayuco tips over again.

When everything is ready, I try to sleep some in the hot sun. My hat is wet and crushed, and it hangs over my head like a rag. It is hard to sleep when I must sit up and also watch the ocean. I worry each moment that something bad will happen. The waves come from the west, and I lean against the paddle to keep the cayuco sailing north. Big wet blisters cover my hands.

As I sail, the shore appears and then disappears

143

again. Late in the day, more garbage floats past the cayuco. I think it is a habit that I have—I look for anything that floats. Today there are only pieces of wood and broken plastic bottles. I find one plastic bottle I can cut and use to empty water.

The sun is almost touching the water when something small and dark floats toward the cayuco. It is nothing I can use, only a little plastic doll that is brown from the sun and water. It has no hair, one arm is missing, and the body is broken almost in half.

But then I look at Angelina staring at the floor. I turn the cayuco very fast so I can grab the doll from the water. "Here, Angelina," I say, giving her the doll.

Angelina takes the doll and stares at it.

"I think the doll is hurt and needs a friend," I say. "Will you help her?"

Angelina turns the doll in her hands and nods. "I think the doll is very hungry," she says.

I open the bottle that soaks the beans, and I take out one bean. "Dolls do not eat very much," I say.

Angelina takes the bean and pushes it into the mouth of the plastic doll. "One is okay," she tells me with a strong voice. "She will not make the coconuts dirty."

With the machete, I chip a small piece of candy loose. I hold out the little piece. "Does your doll like candy?" I ask.

Angelina grabs the candy and pushes it fast into her

own mouth. "No, dolls do not like candy," she says.

I see a piece of palm leaf in the water and grab it. "Maybe you should make the doll a hat," I say.

Angelina nods and takes the palm from my hand.

I smile and try to sleep a little more. Angelina holds her doll and works to make a little hat.

The sun is now gone. I know from the map there is one more big island I will sail past during the night or tomorrow. I hope that I will find more fishnets near the island. Before Angelina lies down to sleep, I tell her, "Angelina, you must sleep with the empty bottles around your chest."

Obediently, she pushes her feet through the loop and pulls it up around her chest. I know the bottles will not be comfortable. I watch Angelina until I think she is asleep, then I, too, let my eyes close to steal sleep from the night.

I wake often as the night begins. The moon has grown each night since we left. Once, when I open my eyes, I find Angelina awake holding the doll in her arms, rocking it and talking to it. I feed her another carrot. I do not think the beans smell very good, but still I eat some. I take one bean and give it to Angelina for her doll. "How is your doll?" I ask.

"I talked to my doll tonight," Angelina says.

"Does your doll talk to you?" I ask.

When Angelina speaks, she whispers. "My doll tells me her family is dead. She tells me she is very scared.

Her body hurts and she is lonely."

"She tells you all those things?" I ask.

Angelina nods.

"Does your doll have a name?"

"Maria," she says.

"Is Maria tired?" I ask.

Angelina yawns. "It is dark and she is very tired."

"Maybe you should sleep with her so she will not be lonely," I say.

Angelina hugs the doll and moves the petate around on the coconuts. It is hard for her to be comfortable sleeping on coconuts with two plastic bottles around her chest. "I will sleep with Maria," she says. "Good night."

"Good night," I say.

"Say good night to Maria," Angelina tells me.

"Good night, Maria," I say.

When Angelina closes her eyes, I begin another long night. As I sail, I watch Angelina sleep. Tonight she does not cry. The light from the shining moon lets me watch her. Both of her arms wrap around the doll, and the look on her face makes me think that her dreams are good dreams.

It is good that I have found Angelina the doll. If I want Angelina to make it to the United States of America, I will need to take very good care of that doll.

20

THE LAST LAND

ONLY A SHORT TIME after I eat the beans, my stomach cramps again and I must sit back over the back of the boat. I stay there a long time until my stomach does not hurt and until there are no more beans left inside me. Angelina does not wake up, but if she does I will tell her I am feeding the fish.

After I use the sleeve to clean myself, I sit back in the seat and make up my mind. I cannot eat the beans if they give me diarrhea and do not make me strong. I understand now why the women in our village cooked beans for a very long time. They did not want to kill their families. Tomorrow I will throw away the soaked beans.

Tonight the waves are only small hills that lift me gently when they pass. The breeze is weak but keeps my sail filled. I wedge the paddle in the notch and sail without holding the paddle.

When the ocean is this way, I do not feel I am moving very fast, but I know the current that hides below me always pushes to the north. Enrique told me that when I leave the Yucatán, this current will separate like two roads, one that flows east and one west. I will sail east.

I think about this to help the hours pass. I also sleep, but not hard. Thoughts drift through my head like a breeze that comes and goes. I know it is never safe to sleep long. But I must sleep, and I think it is better now when the ocean also rests.

Just before the morning comes, small lights flicker far away to my right. I see the lights long before the cayuco carries me close enough to see the land. I think this is the big island the map shows me at the north end of the Yucatán. After this island, I will soon leave all land behind me to cross the Gulf. I pull in the sail a little so the wind will take me closer to shore where I can look for fishing nets.

Again, this morning, luck rides with me in the cayuco. The sun is still below the water when I see a long line of floating balls on the ocean. I lean against the paddle and steer to one of the balls. As I pull close to the net, I watch the shore. I think a fisherman will be very angry if he learns that I steal his fish.

It is wrong for me to steal fish. Mother and Father would also be very angry to know their son, Santiago, steals something that is not his. But I know the fish will save my life. I have no money, I cannot ask permission, and I need to feed Angelina. What else can I do?

This morning, I find three fish in the net. The big fish are still alive. One I throw in the bottom of the cayuco. I will cut it up and eat it when Angelina is awake. The other two, I tie a rope through their mouths and let them drag behind the cayuco. Maybe they will still be good to eat tomorrow.

North of me on the shore, there are the buildings and houses of a big city. Also many white sailing boats float near the island. I do not want to be seen, so I sail away from shore. When the island is only a thin shadow on the water, I let the sail swing wide and I keep sailing north. By now the morning sun is high above the water. Angelina still sleeps with the doll in her arms. She sleeps until the heat comes to the sky like air blowing from a forest that burns. When she wakes up, I try to make her laugh. "Angelina," I say. "Do you want more beans for breakfast?"

Angelina does not speak or laugh. She sticks her tongue out and wrinkles her face until her eyes close.

I laugh. "Okay, I will throw them away," I say. I take the beans that are soaked and throw them into the ocean.

"I hope the beans do not kill the fish," Angelina says.

I rinse the bottle, and this time I soak rice. I hope the rice will taste better and stay in our stomachs. I do not throw away the dry beans still tied in the bag. Maybe they will help me kill pirates.

"Okay, I think we should eat something different," I tell Angelina. "I think we will eat fresh fish." I reach down and lift the fish from the bottom of the cayuco. "Oh, look," I say. "Where did this fish come from?"

Angelina shrugs.

"Did you catch it during the night?"

Angelina thinks. "Maybe I did," she says.

"Maybe it jumped into the boat when we slept because it knew that Angelina was hungry," I say, pulling out the machete.

I know the fish will not stay good in the hot sun, so we eat the raw meat until our stomachs are round. When we finish, I make another notch in the cayuco. Now there are seven notches, and I am very proud of each one. Each is a battle that I have won. I wonder how many more notches the ocean will let me make. I pull out the map and stare for a long time, then I look around me. The big island to my right is already far away and behind me. If I am right, before dark, the mainland will also disappear for the last time to the west. This moment excites me and also scares me.

I am becoming like a grandmother. All day, I worry. What will happen tonight? Do I have enough food? Is every knot tight enough?

To stay busy, I do things on the cayuco to try to prepare for crossing the Gulf. I tie every knot tighter. Angelina pushes the food and the water farther under the deck. I wash Angelina's sore skin with fresh water.

We pull our hats tightly over our heads so the wind cannot blow them away. Angelina ties the little hat she has made to the head of her doll.

Eating the raw fish makes me stronger and lets my mind think. I know that this is the food that will keep us alive. But I have no way to catch fish. And I know a tourist will not sail up to this cayuco and ask to trade our beans for a fishhook.

Later I try to sleep more, but the ocean will not let me. The waves grow bigger, and the swells pass under the cayuco like small mountains that lift us high and then drop us into big valleys. We are so small on this big ocean. To the ocean, I think that I am only a bug. The cayuco is only a floating match, and the sail is nothing but a little leaf. But the cayuco is not afraid. I hope that I can be as brave.

As the land disappears behind me, I do not look back. Now it is time to sail the Gulf. If I look back, I will squint and tell myself that I am seeing the shore. But I will be lying to myself. Thinking I see shore will not help to keep me safe.

Late in the day, when the sun hangs like a big red ball over the water, I finally let myself look back. The shore is gone forever. There is only water as far as the sky.

"Angelina," I say. "Now you must always have the plastic bottles around your chest."

Angelina nods. I think she knows I am scared. Her eyes open wide, and she holds the doll so tight she crushes the head in her little fist.

I force my lips to smile. "Now we start a very great adventure," I say.

Again she nods, but I do not think she understands that we have no choice. The current in the Gulf is too strong to turn back now. Also she does not understand that now each day might be the last day we live. Each night might have no morning.

21

BROKEN LIKE THE DOLL

THE EMPTINESS.

That is what makes the open ocean so hard. Each hour that I sail, I think that I am sailing farther into nothing. It is not like sailing near land where I can look at the shore and know that we move slow or fast, or that we drift this way or that way. Near shore, I know there are other people even if they are bad. But here there is nothing. The current is invisible. Nothing passes the cayuco except the waves, and they change where they go. Behind me, the cayuco stirs the water and tells me I am moving forward. But the ocean is not like a mud puddle that keeps water in one place. The ocean moves, and it does not talk to me. I do not know where the winds and the currents take me. I only pretend I know.

Here on the ocean, I know it will be hard to even know the direction I face. When there is light, I can see my compass. When the sky is clear, I can see the sun and moon and the North Star. But when clouds fill the sky or rains come at night, then I will know only if the wind fills my sail and if I move forward. Then questions will fill my mind and make me think I am lost.

It is not easy to be so alone when you are scared. Every time when I close my eyes, I remember the killing and the red sky. But I also remember the voice of Uncle Ramos. He whispers to me in the dark, "Go as far away as you can and tell what has happened this night." When I hear his voice, it makes me strong again and I keep sailing.

This first night on the open ocean is long, and I do not let myself sleep. When morning comes, we eat another fish and I make another notch in the cayuco. Now I count eight notches. But I have only one fish left.

After we sail half of the day, Angelina starts to talk to me. I think a full stomach makes her forget she is afraid. "Look at the sky," she says.

"Yes," I say. "The clouds look like pieces of ripped cloth."

"And the sun looks like a sun," she says, her face very serious.

I smile.

Early in the afternoon, dark clouds return to the sky. The clouds bring rain and wind again. I do not wait for luck. I let my sail drop early. After I tie the sail, I paddle into the waves. For many hours, I fight the wind and the spray that whips across the deck. My arms are so tired, it is hard to hold my paddle.

When the storm ends, it is almost dark. I am glad to raise the sail again. I am tired, but all is well. Angelina does not cry, and during the rain I have filled one bottle with water. I look at the last fresh fish still dragging behind the cayuco. I will wait until tomorrow to eat this fish and hope that time does not make it bad. The last light from the sun helps me to feed Angelina. She eats a carrot, and three times she fills her mouth with soaked rice.

When Angelina finishes eating, I break off a small piece of candy for her. "This is for my Little Squirrel," I say. "Today, you have played our game very well."

She smiles the way a four-year-old girl should smile, and goes to sleep with both arms wrapped around the little broken plastic doll. When I look at Angelina, I also want to be young again. I want the thoughts in my head to go away with only the hug of a plastic doll.

But my mind still thinks about problems. We do not have enough food. If the last fish is still good in the morning, we must eat all of it before the sun makes it rotten. After that, we will have only a little dried fish and soaked rice left. We also have carrots, coconuts, and four oranges, but all the papaya, sugarcane, and bananas are gone. Again I look down at the sleeping face of Angelina. Her face is happy. I wish that she could stay asleep until this journey ended, but I know that tomorrow she will wake up. She will be sad when her stomach hurts again or when the waves grow big once more.

I am alone with my thoughts as I sail. I know that tonight luck sits beside me in the cayuco. The waves are smaller, and I am able to sleep. I thank the ocean for every moment it is kind to Angelina and me.

For two days the ocean does not change. I sit for long hours and fight the wind, the waves, my memories, and sleep. Nothing changes, except my blisters get bigger and we grow hungrier. My ribs push out from my chest like sticks under my skin. I keep Angelina under the deck, but still her skin dries and burns more each day. Her eyes and cheeks are becoming hollow like a skeleton.

The hot sun hurts us, and always now we are hungry. It feels like a dog is chewing on our stomachs. Angelina sits quiet, her eyes dull, her tongue swollen. I tell her to take care of the doll, but when she is this way, she lets her doll fall between the coconuts.

We are not well, but I know the ocean is not trying to kill us. Except for the heat and being hungry and tired, the ocean has been kind to us. I have made notches number nine and ten in the cayuco. I have also tried to sleep all that I can, because there will be times soon when we will not be able to find sleep.

Luck stays with us until the night after I make the tenth notch. That night begins well. After it is dark, the winds blow stronger and the waves grow, but not so much that I must lower the sail. The moon is bright, and all through the night, the cayuco stays straight and we move fast.

It is almost morning before trouble finds us. By then the waves have become weak and lazy. I am thinking this is good, because now I can close my eyes and sleep.

I will never know all that happens after I close my eyes because my mind does not remember. In the dark, a strange wave makes the cayuco turn. Before I can wake up and paddle, the sail loses air. I do not see the sail pole when it swings hard and hits my head with a loud crack.

There is a bright flash in my head, and then the whole world is tipping. Angelina screams, but the sound means nothing to me. I swing the paddle at the water like a crazy person trying to turn the cayuco, but I do not know what direction I must turn.

My head feels like someone is stepping on my skull. The taste of sweet blood fills my mouth and I spit. I try to think, but my thoughts mix together and when I talk to Angelina, it is like a drunk man trying to speak.

I do not know how the cayuco straightens itself and faces into the waves. Maybe it sails without help, or maybe I help and do not remember it. I think there is a part of my mind that knows what I must do without thinking. Angelina pulls on my hair and screams. I feel her kick me.

The morning sun comes up, but I do not remember

it. There is a loud sound in my ears like the motor of a truck running very fast. I think the truck is driving over my head. Angelina stops crying, and I feel her hands splash water on my face. When this stops, little fingers try to put something into my mouth. Then I throw up.

I am trapped in a world where it hurts to open my eyes and the truck engine fills my head. Still I taste sweet blood, and words cannot leave my throat. There is a voice inside me that tells me I will die if I do not paddle, but I cannot move. I do not feel the blowing of the wind or the crashing of waves. My mind is lost, away from my body in a place deeper than sleep. Maybe I am dying. I feel the heat of the hot sun, and then I am sick again. I keep throwing up, but nothing comes from my stomach.

When my eyes open next, I can only look up and think about one thing at a time. The sky is blue and without clouds. The sun burns my skin. Angelina stares down at me, her cheeks wet from tears. I am lying on the floor of the cayuco, my head leaning back against the seat. I look over the edge of the boat for waves, but there are no waves. Only the gentle lifting and falling of the swells.

"What happened?" I ask, my throat dry. My voice sounds like a frog.

Angelina begins to cry when she hears me speak, but

she does not cry loudly. Words rush from her mouth. "The cayuco almost tipped over many times," she sobs. "You did not move or talk to me all day. You pretended you were dead, but still you breathed. I tried to feed you, but you threw up." Angelina's voice is angry now. "I tried to wash your head, but you would not stop bleeding. You did not help me very much."

"Is that why you kicked me?"

She nods.

Above me the sail hangs loose. I look at the sail pole and I think I know what happened. Carefully I reach my fingers to my head and feel. Blood from a big cut over my right ear covers the right side of my face. Still the truck roars in my ears, and it hurts to open my mouth.

Again I look over the side. I do not understand where the waves are. They have disappeared. The swells are smooth as water in a bay.

"When did the waves leave?" I ask.

"When I shouted at them like you do," Angelina says.

Slowly I pull myself up until I lean against the seat. The ocean is calm, and I hold my head with my hands. "You have taken good care of me," I say, groaning. "You have played our game very well."

Angelina does not smile as she scolds me. "You scared me," she says. "You quit moving like Mama and Papa."

"I am okay," I tell Angelina.

"No, you are broken like my doll," she says.

Again I feel the cut on my head. I lay my head back on the seat and smile a sad smile. "Yes, I am broken like your doll."

22

BAD FISHHOOK

HOW CAN THE OCEAN BE SO CALM today after it tried to kill me yesterday? This question I cannot answer. I know only that I lie still in the bottom of the cayuco and the sun cooks my skin like a tortilla. Above me two small clouds hang without moving, as if someone painted them on the sky. There is no wind. The air moves only enough to flap the sail. Except for the lazy swells that roll past very slowly, the ocean is flat like Lake Izabal in the morning.

I do not know if I should like the calm ocean or hate it. There is more time to think and to heal, but also more time for the sun and hunger to try and kill us. Maybe it is better to fight an angry ocean. Then if we live or if we die, the end comes quickly.

All I know is that today, I am glad the ocean does not fight me. My head is cracked open like a coconut. Even now, blood leaks down across my cheek. I wipe at it with the piece of shirt I still wear. My hat keeps the sun off my face but not off my body. My feet reach under the deck. Angelina sits above me on the seat.

When I sit up late in the afternoon, I count ten notches in the cayuco. I pick up the machete and make one more. Swinging a big knife is not safe when I cannot think well, but this is very important to me. Now the cayuco has eleven notches.

"What do we eat?" Angelina asks.

I know she is hungry, but my head cannot think to answer her.

"What do we eat?" she asks louder.

"Anything," I say.

Angelina digs in my pocket for the candy.

"No!" I grunt.

"But you said I can eat anything," she argues.

I do not answer her, and she crawls under the deck. She knows I cannot argue. When she comes back into the sun, she carries the two dried fish. These are not big fish, and they have much salt covering them.

"Scrape the salt off," I say. "The salt will only make us very thirsty." I know that these fish are the best food that we have left, but maybe now is a good time to eat one.

Angelina holds the machete between her knees and pulls the fish across the sharp blade to scrape off the salt. I know it is not safe for a little girl to use a machete, but

I cannot move to help her. With great care, she pulls the fish apart. For a long time she picks at the bones with her fingers and pokes food into both of our mouths. She even sucks on the dried head to make sure there is nothing more that she can eat.

The fish tastes good, and I can think and sit all the way up on the floor when we are finished eating. But I know that now we have even less food. All we have left is one more fish, a few oranges and carrots, the small bag of rice, and a little candy. That is only enough food for two or maybe three more days. I do not know what I will do then.

We still have the coconuts, but chewing on coconuts only makes us more thirsty. Because of the hot sun, we have used much water and have little left. Until it rains again, I cannot let Angelina drink very much, even if her lips are dry, cracked, and swollen. I decide we can eat coconuts only after we find more water.

"Fish can fly," Angelina tells me.

"No," is all I say, because it hurts to talk.

"Yes," she says. "This morning, when you did not want to wake up, I saw fish fly over the boat."

Because I am older than Angelina, I know that fish do not fly. Maybe it is sea gulls that she sees. "Catch one," I tell her.

"Okay," she says, her voice stubborn.

Eating gives Angelina more strength, and she crawls around me in the boat. I do not let her crawl on top of the deck, but she sits behind me on the seat, holding the paddle like she is sailing. Still she wears the water bottles around her chest. She has moved both bottles around to her back, so she looks like a little angel with big fat wings sitting above me.

When Angelina crawls past me to go under the deck, her hat and the bottles hit me, but I do not want to say angry words to her. It is good that she is moving, and I think this will help her skin. Both of us have many sores now that do not heal. When Angelina sits still, she scratches at her wet sores and picks the scabs off the dry ones.

I do not know why Angelina crawls around and talks today when I am hurt. Yesterday she sat very quietly. Maybe she knows she must be strong and help me. I lean against the seat with my eyes closed.

"Look," she shouts. "More flying fish."

I do not open my eyes or answer her, because I need to sleep.

When I wake up, it is dark. Angelina is asleep beside me with her head on my shoulder. Still there are no waves or wind. It is like the sky holds its breath. Or maybe it is taking a deep breath so tomorrow it can blow harder. I look up. The black sky is like a dark blanket that is pulled over me. The stars make a thousand little holes in that blanket. I close my eyes again and fall asleep. Because the ocean is calm, I sleep harder than any night since the sky turned red over my village.

When morning comes, my body does not want to

wake up. I hear and I feel Angelina crawling near me. She talks more about flying fish. This does not stop my sleep. When I finally open my eyes, the sun has already made the air hot. Angelina sits behind me on the seat. She lifts the hat that she has laid across my face and giggles. The bright sun hurts my eyes, and I squint.

I learn why Angelina giggles. She holds a small silver-blue fish in her hand. She sits above me and lets the fish touch my nose.

I push the fish away and grunt, "Where did you get that fish?"

"I said that fish fly, but you did not believe me. This one flew into the boat."

My muscles hurt but I sit up. I do not want to play a game this morning. "It did not fly," I say. "It jumped in."

Angelina shakes her head. "Look," she says. She holds the fish up and spreads out long thin fins from behind the head. The fins spread in her fingers like wings.

Me, I do not want to argue, but I am still thinking in my mind that a fish does not fly. Then behind me, there are splashes.

"See the fish fly!" Angelina screams.

I turn and stare. Small fish are jumping from the calm water. After they jump, their silver wings flutter, and the fish fly far through the air before splashing back into the ocean. One fish flies across the boat.

I do not know what to say. What else does the ocean

have that is magic? Maybe I will believe Angelina the next time she speaks.

I cut the flying fish into thin pieces with the machete. The fish is not big, but it is soft and easy to swallow. The meat is almost sweet. When we finish, we eat one orange. The candy is almost gone because the salt water has melted it away. Still I break off a small piece. "This is for you, Angelina," I say. "Because you have saved my life today."

"Does that mean I am playing our game well?"

I smile. "Yes, that means you are playing our game very well."

After we eat, we drink only a little water because the meat of the fish is already wet and helps us. We will need the water later. Now it is time to cut another notch in the cayuco. This is the only time each day that I enjoy, because I can count the notches. Each notch means we have survived another day. This morning I count the notches aloud with Angelina helping me. Our voices grow louder and louder with each number until we almost shout the number twelve.

But what will happen during day number thirteen? My head still hurts and I am weak. We have very little food and water left. And soon the winds and the waves will be strong again. Because we cannot catch fish now, I think that maybe we will die soon. It is only luck that lets a flying fish land in the boat.

Sitting in the seat, I try to make my sore head think.

All around me there is food. Even now small fish swim under the cayuco. I swing the paddle at them, but they are too fast. They know I do not have a hook.

Slowly I look around the boat. Maybe it is possible to make a hook. I see the shells Angelina brought from the island of the pirates. I hold the biggest shell in my fingers and look at it. Angelina watches me as I use the machete and start to cut and chip at the shell. She holds out her doll. "Can Maria help you?"

"Yes," I say. "Maria must tell me if I do something wrong."

All day I work to make a hook. The sun above me is like a great fire burning. The calm water is a mirror that burns us.

When the machete slips and cuts my finger, Angelina speaks. "Maria says, 'Do not cut your finger.'"

"Thank you," I say, and keep working.

At last I finish making a rough shell hook. The fishing line pushes hard through the small hole, but finally I tie a strong knot. It is almost dark when I break off a small piece of dried fish and press it over the hook. I hold up the line like a great prize. "I am ready," I say.

Angelina's eyes are silent as I lower the hook and dried fish into the water. "Maria says you should let the hook go deeper," she whispers.

"Okay," I whisper back. I smile and let the hook sink deeper. Maybe Maria is right.

We do not wait long before a fish bites the hook. The

line tightens in my hand, and I feel a hard pull. Then the line falls loose again. Slowly I raise the line from the water.

The shell hook is broken. All the work of one day is gone in one second, and I want to cry. It is cruel for the ocean to tease someone this way before it kills them.

Angelina speaks with a voice that is very serious. "Maria tells me that you did not make a very good fishhook."

23

THE NAIL

I AM NUMB with anger as I look out across the still dark water. It is not fair that I should work so hard all day to make something that breaks so soon. The shell hook did not catch even one fish. Inside, I feel empty. Is the ocean playing with me the way a cat plays with a mouse before death?

"It is time for sleep," I tell Angelina.

She does not argue, but her body is not ready for sleep. When she curls up beside me, she rolls and moves. For many hours, she keeps rolling and moving. Her little elbows and knees dig into my side like the coconuts and the handle of the paddle.

I try not to say angry words. "Lie very still so your doll can sleep," I say.

"She is already sleeping," Angelina whispers.

My body hurts and my eyes want to cry as we float on

the calm ocean. All through the night, I keep waking. It is hard to know when my thoughts are real or only dreams. Above me the moon hangs like a big tortilla. I do not know if I will ever stand on land and see this moon again.

It is still dark when a silent wind comes over the water to make the sail flap harder. The sail pole swings and bumps against the mast. Again waves rock the cayuco. The change is small and very gentle, so I sleep again. But when morning comes, the wind is strong enough to fill the sail. My head hurts as I yawn and try to think.

This is when I first see the movement. It is like the shadow of a cloud passing beside the cayuco, but there is no cloud above me. The shadow becomes darker. I look into the water and my breath stops.

I do not know the animals of the ocean well, so I do not know what is beside me. Uncle Ramos has shown me pictures of whales and sharks. The thing that glides beside me in the water is too big to be a shark, and I do not think it is a whale. The shadow comes closer to the cayuco, and then a fin breaks above the water. Now I can see the head, and it *is* a shark. This shark is bigger than any shark from even my dreams. The cayuco is almost seven meters long, and the shark is as long as two cayucos. I remember now Uncle Ramos telling me of these giant sharks.

The shark hangs beside me like it is thinking. One

eye looks at me. Now I too am thinking. Does the shark want to eat me? Maybe it waits to grow hungry. I decide I will not hit the shark with the paddle. I think a hungry shark is better than one that is angry.

I let my eyes look out across the water. The ocean makes me feel small because it is so big. As far as my eyes can see, there is only water, and this is only the top of the ocean. Below there is a world I do not know. This great animal that moves beside the cayuco is a part of that world. I know it can kill me if it wants, but today it does not kill me. Instead it moves its big tail two times and, like a shadow, it disappears into the black deep.

Angelina still sleeps. When she wakes, I will not tell her about the shark. There are many things I do not tell Angelina, because I do not think a child should be afraid. Until she wakes, I look at the map, and I look at the compass. Because there is no land, I can only guess where I am. Uncle Ramos has told me that sailors know where they are by the position of the stars. I do not know these things. All I know is that I am hungry.

This is how another day comes and goes. I make notch number thirteen. Angelina and I eat a little rice and one carrot, and we both take a bite of salted fish. Angelina tries to take a big bite. This little food and water will be all we eat today. I am afraid of the time when I must tell Angelina there is no more water or food.

All day the sun hangs above the cayuco and burns us. The wind and the waves grow, but today they are not my enemy. Today my enemy is the hunger, the heat, and being alone. Also the sun and salt make more sores and blisters on our bodies. The blisters, some as big as my hand, bubble up and bleed. They leave ugly open wounds on our backs and arms and legs. The bleeding sores grow on our bodies and burn like fire when salt water wets them.

I give Angelina the last small piece of candy, but the taste does not last long in her mouth. She wants coconut milk. I shake my head. Angelina cries because she hurts, and so I use the coconut milk to wet her sores. I think it helps her. Or maybe it is only because that is what she believes.

Drunk with hunger and pain, we sail into the next night and into the next day. It is the afternoon of day number fourteen when clouds come to the sky. At last the sun cannot reach through the clouds to burn us. But these clouds are dark and reach down to stir the water with wind that beats the sail. I do not understand how yesterday the ocean slept, clear and flat and calm as the top of a table, but now it grows dark as the sky, with foam that spits at me.

The rain comes first, with big drops that hit my skin like hard beans. "Crawl under the deck," I tell Angelina. The rain falls harder. Soon it is like being under a waterfall. I do not waste the rain. First I fill the water bottles and we drink. Then I tell Angelina, "Come, and we will wash."

She shakes her head, but I pull her with a strong hand into the rain. Her dirty red dress is no more than a rag hanging from her shoulders now, but I let the rain wash it while I rub the sores that cover her arms and legs and body. I run my fingers through Angelina's matted hair. She takes deep breaths and screams, but she does not fight me. She knows that this will help her.

After I have cleaned Angelina, I do the same to my body. The pain when I rub salt from my open sores makes me close my eyes and bite my teeth. This is the same pain that made Angelina scream. I look at the bottles tied to her chest. It is best if they stay empty. The bottles I have filled will last for a few days if we are careful.

The wind stays strong, but because it pushes me from behind, I leave the sail up. The rest of this day and night, I do not sleep. Always the waves and wind try to turn the cayuco to the side. When I sail like this, I am not afraid of the waves that follow me and let me know when they are near. What scares me is the waves that travel alone. There are waves that come from any direction and do not warn me before they attack the cayuco. I think they come to kill. That is what tipped the cayuco before, and maybe that is what made the sail pole swing and hit me. All night I look out over the black water and wait for one of these killers.

When morning number fifteen comes, I am glad to make another notch. I look at all my notches. If the cayuco does not reach the United States of America, how many more notches will I make before I die? My body grows weaker each day, and each day the ocean kills us a little more.

Today, day number fifteen, I know the food is almost gone. There are only two oranges, a little fish, and some rice for tomorrow and maybe the next day. Because we have water, I let Angelina eat coconut. But later, her hunger is even worse. She holds her stomach and cries. I hear the pain in her voice and know she will die if I cannot catch a fish.

Again I try to find something to make a hook. The nails used to build the cayuco are too big. I look over the barrel guard at the deck boards Enrique nailed on. These nails are also big, but I see two small nails he used near the mast.

I do not like climbing over the deck when the waves are big and I am weak. I start to tie a loose rope around my waist but then decide this can trip me. No, I have no choice. Staying alive does not mean I can always be safe. I need one of those nails. "Angelina, sit down and hold on to the side," I say.

She sits, and I untie the machete from the cayuco. I do not dare lose the machete, so I tie it to my wrist. When I cannot see any big waves, I climb fast over the barrel guard and crawl on my knees to the mast. I dig at one of the small nails with the tip of the machete.

When each wave rolls past us, I wait to see if the cayuco will keep straight for the next wave. If it turns, I climb back to the seat and paddle like a crazy person so that we do not tip. This is stupid what I am doing. If I fall into the water, I cannot stop the cayuco. It will sail away with Angelina faster than I can swim.

Each time I crawl forward over the deck, Angelina yells, "Come back!"

"I will!" I answer and dig faster around the nail. Again and again I crawl back to the seat when the cayuco turns. Finally the nail moves in the wood. My knees bleed and my arms are weak. I see a big wave coming, so I grab the top of the nail and pull hard. The nail cuts my fingers, but it twists free. I put the nail in my mouth as I climb back to the seat holding the machete.

The wave almost tips the cayuco on its side, but I am able to turn at the last moment. I take the small nail from my mouth and look at it. I have risked much for this little piece of metal. Now I must make a fishhook.

24

I CAN CATCH A FISH

LIFE DOES NOT ALWAYS GIVE a person a teacher when one is needed. That is what I am thinking when I look at the nail. Somehow a fishhook can be made, but how? I must find the answer inside of me. Even now my body wants to stop and my mind does not want to think. If I do not catch a fish by tomorrow, I will grow too weak to sail the cayuco.

I hit the back of the machete against the small piece of metal. It is hard to hold the nail against the seat between my legs. My fingers are numb. Even when the machete makes a deep cut in my thumb, I keep working. Blood covers my fingers, the nail, the machete, and drips onto the seat. Each time I hit with the machete, the nail turns in my fingers and digs into the wood. Once I drop the nail and think it is lost in the water, but I find it and keep hitting until the end bends around like a hook.

As I work, I keep looking up for the next wave. Angelina sits under the deck and watches me. She holds her doll by the leg.

When I work like this, I do not know how much time passes. I see nothing now except the nail, the machete, the paddle, and the next wave. This is all that exists in the world. And always my mouth is dry, and the truck motor echoes in my hurting head. Every move I make is because I am very scared. If I lose this nail, I am too weak to pull out another one. This I know.

Finally I have a hook but it is not sharp. To make it sharp, I need something hard to rub against the nail. Moving very slowly so I do not drop the nail, I rub the hook along the side of the machete. Soon the long blade is covered with blood but I keep rubbing. Angelina watches with dull, empty eyes.

All of my fingers bleed before the small hook is finally sharp. I sit and stare at the hook. My body is weak and needs food. I give Angelina a little bite of salted fish and half an orange. I eat the other half and also take a bite of the fish. When Angelina is not looking, I take another bite of the fish. I am bigger and must work harder. If I am not strong, we will both die.

The sky is dark when we drink water and finish our small meal. Because the sun has gone down, I will wait until morning to fish. I am so tired I cannot think. It would be too easy to drop the hook or line at night.

"I am still hungry," Angelina cries.

"I am, too," I say. I give Angelina another drink of water, but her tears do not stop.

I think this night is my longest night on the ocean. Other nights, each moment seemed to last an hour. Tonight, each moment seems to last the night, and each hour is a lifetime. My body grows so weak that I cannot hold back my tears.

Tonight, it is not enough to sit in the cayuco and wait for morning. Tonight, I fight each minute of darkness like my enemy. Each moment becomes a battle that is won or lost, and this night I do not dare lose even one battle. If I sleep, the ocean will try to kill me again. I decide that tomorrow morning, when I cut the notch for another day, the notch will be so big maybe the boat will fall in half. But cutting the notch in the cayuco is only a thought that keeps me awake. When morning light does find the sky, I am too weak to swing the machete.

Now I am like a dead person. When Angelina wakes up and looks at me, her eyes tell me she is scared of what she sees. I think it is good I cannot look into a mirror. My ribs poke out and I am smeared with blood from making the hook and from fighting a battle against the ocean. My body is covered with sores, and I think my eyes sink deep into my head. I try to smile, but all I can do is stare at Angelina with a hollow stare. My mind does not work right.

Today I need to be strong, so I eat the last of the dried fish with Angelina. I save only a little that I can use for bait. I drink water and then take the small fish-hook from my pocket. The line is wrapped around a stick that I have pushed under the seat where it cannot come loose.

I move with much care so that I do not make a mistake as I pull the end of the line through my fingers. The waves are still big, but they do not curl at the top. This morning the smell of salt is strong in my nose. I wrap the line around the head of the nail and tie a knot. The bait will hide the flat head.

When I am ready, there is no excitement, only the shaking of my hand. I am weak and scared. This is my last chance. Everything must be right or we will die. I pull a small piece of fish over the hook, then lower the line into the waves. I cannot see below the water because the ocean is not calm now. The waves are bigger, so I let the line sink more. This is what my mind thinks is right.

Now all I can do is look into Angelina's scared eyes and wait. She knows that what we do is very important. I hold the line out away from my body. Because the hook is smooth, it will let a fish come off if I do not keep the line tight.

A long time passes without a bite. Finally I rest my tired hand on the edge of the cayuco. Maybe the fish do not bite when the waves are high. Maybe they do not eat salted fish. Maybe the fish can see my hook and think I am a very stupid fisherman that does not know how to catch even a floating log. My mind thinks this way when it is tired. I want to sleep.

Then the line pulls in my hand. I pull back hard, but there is no fish. Now my mind pushes sleep away, and I hold my hand back out. The next pull comes quickly. This time I do not jerk. I only pull to keep the hook holding the fish. It is not a very big fish, but I pull the line carefully, hand over hand, toward the cayuco.

I can see the small silver fish in the water. It is like a streak of light that races under the waves. I hold my breath and pull the fish toward me. In the air, it wiggles hard and falls free, back into the ocean. Before I can think, the fish is gone.

I want to cry. Why do I waste my time trying to fish? If I put the paddle at my feet and close my eyes, the cayuco will float sideways to the next big wave and the ocean will soon end my struggle and pain. But I see Angelina, and she stares at me. I am all that she has. She believes that I will save her.

I pull another small piece of salted fish over the hook and lower the line into the water. This time I wait much longer before a fish bites, but it is a bigger fish. Already I know what I will do when it comes close to the cayuco. I pull very carefully. When there is a flash of silver beside me, I give a hard pull toward the boat that brings the fish fast out of the water. The fish struggles and comes off the hook, but this time it lands in the bottom of the cayuco.

I want to shout and scream, but I am too weak. It takes all of my strength to pull in the fish line and place it under the seat. I will fish more later, but now we must eat. My hands are clumsy when I hold the fish. I take the machete and chop the fish in the back of the neck. The body quivers, then the eyes become dull and it stops moving. I cut the head off. The fish drips blood. Angelina pulls on my arm so that I will squeeze fish blood into her small mouth.

Then I cut the fish and we eat. We do not stop eating until there is nothing left that a person can eat. We chew on the head and eat even the eyeballs. Then I take the machete and I cut another notch in the cayuco. There are sixteen notches now.

"You can catch a fish," Angelina says, her words simple but strong.

"Yes, I can catch a fish," I say. "We are hurt like the doll, but the ocean does not break us. We are strong like this little cayuco."

25

THE STORM

THE FISH makes us stronger. My body wakes as if from death, and my mind can think again. I know Angelina is better because she complains. She does not like the plastic bottles tied to her chest. She does not like the waves. She is hungry. She cries and scratches at her cracked and bleeding sores. The sun is hot, but she does not want to wear her hat. The hats that she made are now crushed and broken and rotted by the salt water. Still, we must throw them over our heads and shoulders like mats.

"Angelina," I say. "You do not play our game very well if you complain."

"I hate our game," she tells me. Her voice is stubborn and angry. "You do not give me candy anymore."

"There is no more candy," I say. "So, what should I do?"

"I want to go home," she says.

"The soldiers burned our home," I say.

"I want Mama and Papa and Anita and Rolando and Arturo," she says.

I take a deep breath because I do not know if what I say is good for a four-year-old girl to hear. Candy cannot take the hurt away from my next words. "Angelina," I say. "The soldiers have killed all of them."

Angelina turns and hits my knee with her small fist. Then she covers her ears with her hands. "I do not hear you," she says.

"Okay, I will not talk," I say.

We sail for a long time. I think many thoughts as I look ahead at the ocean. Angelina looks down at her knees, her hands still over her ears. She peeks up at me, but I pretend not to see her.

Suddenly Angelina kicks me. "I hate you if you do not talk to me," she says.

"Okay, I will talk," I say. "But you must take your hands off your ears."

Very slowly, Angelina drops her hands to her knees.

"Angelina," I say. "Something very bad is happening to you and me. I am scared like you. I am also hungry and hot. My body hurts, and I am very tired. But if we complain and give up, we will die." I wait so Angelina will understand my words well. "Do you want to die?" I ask.

Angelina stares at me, then shakes her head slowly. "But I hurt," she says. Her voice is scared.

"Where does it hurt the most?" I ask.

183

She points to her heart. "Inside here."

Angelina's words make tears come to my eyes. "Yes, that is where I hurt, too," I say. "But we cannot give up. I do not know where we are, but we must believe that we are close to land. I know when the weather is bad we cannot fish, so you must help me today. We will catch more fish and cut the meat into little pieces. The sun is hot. I think it will dry the meat before it becomes bad. We will have fish to eat later."

"What can I do?" Angelina asks.

"You can help me hang up the meat. Okay?"

Angelina nods. "You need to catch fish first."

I wipe the tears from my eyes and let my cracked lips smile a tired smile. "Yes, I will need to catch fish first." I reach under the seat and pull out the fishing line and the hook.

"Hurry," Angelina says.

I pretend to hurry, but I move with great care. On the ocean, mistakes are not forgiven. The first fish I catch is very small, and I throw it under the seat to use as bait. The next fish comes off the hook before I pull it from the water.

"Fish better," Angelina says.

I try to fish better, but even when I am more careful, many fish fight and come loose from the hook. The few fish that I do catch are small, but still I cut these up and make thin strips. In each strip of meat I cut a hole. Angelina pushes a thin rope through this hole. When she first starts, I think she eats more fish than she hangs. She also pushes little pieces of fish into the mouth of her broken doll, Maria. I do not scold her. It is good that she thinks she is helping. If luck will also help us, maybe we will catch a bigger fish.

Each time after I catch a fish, I check the line where it ties to the hook. If the line is worn, I tie it again. I do not dare lose the hook.

"Catch me a big fish," Angelina says. "Then I can hang up more meat."

I do not answer. Does she think I tell the hook what to catch?

But maybe the hook hears her words. The next fish I catch is big. Angelina reaches to grab the pieces of meat before I finish cutting. Now luck decides to help me. Angelina is still hanging pieces of meat when I catch a second big fish. I think fresh bait helps us. I cut up this meat and keep fishing.

When the rope hangs heavy with meat, I tie it high on the mast. It is like a clothesline that dries clothes. Because I tie the rope high, I hope the wind will also help the meat to dry.

It is late in the day when I cut up the last fish. I am tired and my body hurts, but I feel hope again. Hope is something that hunger and big waves have almost robbed from us. I know it is good what we have done today.

As night comes to the sky, the little cayuco pushes

ahead. It meets each new wave with a big splash. I hope that tonight I can be as strong as this small boat. I think I can. I am beginning this night on the open ocean with a full stomach. Today we have played our game of staying alive very well.

Already the meat is dried enough by the sun that it will not become bad, but still I leave the fish hanging so it can dry even more during the night. I wrap up the fishing line. Before I push it under the seat, I hold the small fishhook in my hand and look at it. I am very proud. Luck did not make this hook.

Tomorrow I will fish more if the waves let me. Tonight sleep comes and goes from my head. Always I am scared of the big waves that travel alone. I make sure that Angelina has her empty water bottles around her chest. I do not think she understands how the bottles will save her life. She thinks it is something I do to punish her.

This night is long, but I do not think anything can be worse than last night. Tonight I let myself eat dried fish. It is hard to chew, but it makes me strong and helps to keep me awake.

When morning comes, I am ready again to fish. I make another notch. I help Angelina count the notches. I let her discover what I already know. Now the cayuco has seventeen notches.

I look at the notches, and I wonder when we will see land. Uncle Ramos told me it would take maybe twenty days. Now my mind thinks only of that number, but I know that maybe we will arrive sooner and maybe we will arrive later. I know we cannot live long enough to arrive much later.

This day we catch more fish. Again I let Angelina eat all the fish she wants. In the afternoon dolphins come beside the cayuco. For a long time they share the ocean with us as they jump and roll across the waves. Finally they leave, but Angelina and I talk about them until the stars come to the sky.

"The dolphins came to see me," Angelina says.

"Yes, I think that is true," I say.

"They smile and are happy," she says.

"Yes, they smile and are happy," I say.

"I wish I was a dolphin," Angelina says.

The next three days come and go.

Each morning the hot sun begins a cruel climb into another sky without clouds. Each night stars fill the black night, and we follow the North Star. Always I am tired, but each hour I find some sleep. We fish until there is no more room to hang fish on the cayuco. I know that soon we will need water again. I tell Angelina we must take only small drinks.

With full stomachs, time passes more quickly. I can count notches number eighteen and nineteen. The morning I make notch number twenty in the cayuco, I look hard across the water, as if at this moment I will see land. I want to cry when I see only ocean in every direction.

I have stayed brave by promising myself that in twenty days we will reach land. But I know the ocean currents and the winds do not listen to my hopes and dreams and promises. Maybe we have drifted away from our course. Maybe the ocean has already decided it is going to let us die.

I have no choice but to keep sailing. Two more days and two more nights pass. Now Angelina and I are lost on an empty ocean, unable to sleep, burned by the hot sky, and carried by winds and currents toward a place that maybe is not real. Maybe the United States of America is only a dream. Our lips are cracked and hard. Our tongues are dry and swollen in our mouths. When I wipe my cracked lips, there is blood on my hand. I stare at the blood, but what can I do?

I do not tell Angelina what I am thinking. Even with fish to eat, I feel the end of our lives coming. Each hour it is harder to move and to think. The sores eat at our bodies like big insects. My body is so weak now, it does not always do what I want. Angelina no longer speaks. She curls her body under the deck and stares with an empty look at the floor. We have no more water, so we must drink milk from the coconuts. The milk is good to swallow but always we have diarrhea. This only makes our sores worse and brings back our thirst.

I do not think we can live more than one or two

more days. This makes me mad. I think that the ocean is a coward. If it will fight me, I will fight back. But the waves do not grow smaller, and they do not grow bigger. Nothing changes, except our bodies grow weaker.

It is the night after I make notch number twenty-two that the ocean grows tired of waiting. Maybe now it thinks we are weak enough to kill. In the middle of the night, the stars disappear. By morning all of the sky above me is filled with clouds. The clouds are not white blankets high in the sky. These are dark heavy clouds that roll over the ocean with big bellies that hang down almost to the water. They bring with them winds that grab and beat the sail.

I know a bad storm is coming, and so I work hard to make everything ready. Big raindrops hit the deck as I roll the dried fish into the sleeping mat. I push the roll of fish far under the deck. I tie all the knots well and make sure the sail is ready to bring down.

It is the middle of the day, and I am still making the cayuco ready when something happens I do not understand. The wind stops, and the air becomes hot and still. The waves do not change, but the air feels heavy. For a long time it is like this, then the wind begins to blow again. Now it blows stronger and the swells grow until they are great mountains of ocean that pass under me. I loosen the knot from the seat and lower the sail. This is good, because soon the waves turn white and carry patches of foam on their backs like big shaggy monsters.

"Sit down on the coconuts," I tell Angelina. "And hold on to the deck hard."

Angelina obeys. She holds the deck with one hand, and she holds her doll with the other hand.

Spray stings my face as I fight to tie the sail to the sail poles. Now foam blows across the swells in long streaks. When the front of the cayuco hits a wave, spray and foam crash across the top of the deck and into my face. The wind whips the ocean. It takes water from the top of the waves and sprays it through the air like an angry cloud.

Now, without a sail, I paddle hard. The brave little cayuco pushes forward, fighting to climb the face of one big wave until I feel it balance at the top, and then we rush down the other side into the face of another wave. The wind blows so hard, the rain drives sideways like bullets across the deck.

There is something new and angry in this air that I have not known before. No longer does the ocean rise and fall with a rhythm. These waves do not follow each other. They come at the cayuco from every direction like great, angry walls of water. When the waves crash into each other, it is as if they want to fight. The waves hiss and suck like evil monsters.

I do not know which way to turn the cayuco. We are attacked from every side. The waves pound me as if I am their enemy. The water crashing across the deck is pulling the deck boards loose. I know if they come off, the cayuco will fill with water. But I can do nothing. I look for the next wave and paddle even harder, breathing fast with fear.

And then it happens. I am paddling hard to meet one wave when I hear a roar and look to my right. Another wave, bigger than a truck, already lifts the cayuco from the side. The front of the wave is a big wall of water that curls over me from the top. There is no time to turn into the wave. The cayuco lifts like a small leaf.

I know what is happening, and I grab Angelina by her arm. With the other hand I hold on to the side. "We are tipping over!" I scream.

When the cayuco tips over, it is not something that happens fast. It tips slowly onto its side as if a big hand has pushed it down. Angelina and I fall into the water. When my head breaks above the surface to breathe, I look up at the big wave. It still hangs above us, deciding what to do.

"Hold on to me!" I scream to Angelina.

I hold her, and I feel her arms squeeze my neck. I see that she is still holding her doll as the ocean falls on us.

26

STARS ON THE WATER

AS THE WAVE crashes down on us, I grab the cayuco, but it is ripped from my hand. Then the world explodes and we are underwater. We roll and turn and cannot breathe. Big hands of water pull and push against us. I hold my breath. Angelina's little body struggles in my arm, but I hold her tight to my chest. When my head breaks above the waves, I gasp for air and grab the cayuco again. Fear and water choke me. And then we are underwater once more.

Another wave crashes over the cayuco before I can find more air. This time I am able to hold on. Something snaps, and I see the mast break in the middle. Angelina screams and chokes on water. I do not let go of her. I am holding the side of the cayuco near the seat. From under the deck, everything we have floats out into the ocean. All around the cayuco there are coconuts and water bottles. The dried fish floats past us, and I can only watch.

A wave tries to pull me away from the cayuco, but I will not let go. The ocean can take all of my food and all of my water, but I will not give it my life so easily.

The empty bottles tied around Angelina's chest hold her above the water. The wind screams, and Angelina screams. I do not know which one screams louder. Between waves, I reach and pull us forward to where I can hold on to the deck. When I do this, I push one foot under the deck to keep the waves from pulling me away. Now it is easier to hold Angelina, and the barrel guard helps protect us from the spray.

The cayuco rolls and twists in the angry ocean, but it cannot tip any farther. All of the lines are broken and tangled. The ripped sail spreads itself on the water and keeps the cayuco from rolling when big waves wash over us. The broken mast hits against the deck. There is nothing I can do but hold on. Still Angelina screams.

"I am holding you!" I yell at Angelina, but my words are lost in the wind. I think only time will quiet my sister.

And I am right. After I hold Angelina for a long time beside the cayuco, finally her screams soften to lonely cries. More time passes, and these cries become hiccups that grab at her chest. I feel sorry for Angelina, and I feel sorry for myself now. There is nothing more I can do but let the storm blow around us until we cannot hold on anymore. And then? I do not like to think about then. Then we will lose our game.

The low clouds that roll past touch the tops of the waves. Swells rise and fall like the chest of a great animal. The ocean is alive and it breathes. When the ocean breathes, wind whistles over the waves and grabs at us. Each time another big wave crashes into the cayuco, it takes another breath of my hope. I know now that the ocean does not care. It does not care when it takes my food and my water, and it does not care now if it kills a scared boy and his little sister.

My shoulders grow numb from holding on for so long. My hands bleed, and salt-water spray stings my eyes. It feels like hours since we have tipped over, but still the storm screams around us like big cats fighting in the sky. I take a loose piece of rope and tie Angelina to the cayuco. I am too weak to hold her anymore. Still she holds her broken doll tight in her fist.

I do not know how long the storm blows or for how long I hold on to the side of the cayuco. Time has disappeared again. The sky grows darker, but I do not know if the storm grows worse or if night has come. I think it is night that has come because the wind does not scream so loud anymore. The waves do not attack me.

I look at Angelina. The rope cuts deep into the skin of her chest, and her face is the face of a ghost. She looks at me with eyes that have no feelings except haunted fear.

"Do not give up!" I scream. "The storm is ending!" Angelina's empty eyes only blink at me.

I wait until the wind and the waves lose their anger before I crawl out onto the sideboard and pull the cayuco upright. It is dark now, and the sky is black. Because the mast is broken in the middle, the cayuco tips upright with one hard pull. I lift Angelina aboard.

I do not know what to do now. The ripped sail flaps like a loose sheet from the broken mast. Everything is gone, the coconuts, the fish, the water, the machete, everything. I feel under the seat. Even the fishhook and line are gone. The only thing still tied to the cayuco is the paddle, and it is broken.

Like a machine, I scoop water from the cayuco with my hands, even if my arms do not want to move. I do not know why I do this. Maybe it is because my mind knows nothing but our game. Maybe staying alive is a game that all people play. Maybe it is the only game that anybody really knows. Even now when death sits beside me in the cayuco, I pretend to play the game one last time.

When my arms need to rest, I sit and stare out across the dark water. I do not paddle very hard to meet the next wave, because I have no more strength and because my heart has lost all hope. If a wave tips me over now, this will be the end. A candle does not burn when there is no wax left.

It is now, as I stare across the dark waves with all hope lost, that I first see the flicker of lights. They bounce above the waves, and I think they are only stars. But clouds still hide the stars, and stars do not look like a string of lights that float on the waves. My mind does not want to understand what I am seeing, because already it has given up. I blink my eyes again and again but the lights do not disappear. My breath catches in my chest.

"Angelina, look," I say.

Angelina does not look up. She lies on the floor of the cayuco. I know her body is not dead because her chest still moves, and she still holds the broken doll tight in her fist. Nothing, not even a storm or tipping over, has made her let go of her doll.

I see the lights, but I am too weak to paddle. The waves and the wind blow from behind me and push me forward. I cannot tell how far away I am, but that does not matter. I must not give up. With weak arms, I lift the broken paddle and drop it into the water. I do not think this helps to push the cayuco very much, but hope makes me try.

For a long time, I do not think the lights come any closer. Maybe they are only a dream. But slowly the bright lights stretch farther and farther along the shore. After more time, I can see that this is a very big city. Nowhere in Guatemala are there so many lights. The lights ahead of me keep my arms moving. I do not let my mind think that this is the United States of America. These lights are only the dream of somebody who is almost dead. Yes, this is only a dream. But it is a good dream. I keep paddling, because I do not want this dream to end.

I do not know how much more time passes before the shadow of the shore appears. Now I have stopped paddling. The waves take me toward a stone wall that reaches out from shore. I try to paddle again, but my arms do not obey me. A man stands on the wall and stares at me as I float past him. I let the wind and the waves carry the cayuco forward. Everywhere there are lights. I hear music and people talking and shouting. There are the sounds of motors and horns.

Ahead, there is one building with brighter lights than the others. Many people are walking along the beach. I force my arms to move the paddle. The cayuco drifts forward. Lights shine across the water like long tangled ribbons. With a weak voice that does not sound like mine, I say, "Look, Angelina. Look at the lights."

Angelina still does not lift her head to look.

Now people on the beach turn to look at the cayuco that floats toward them out of the dark. Some of them point. Still I try to pull at the water with the paddle. I must not stop. But each stroke feels like my last. And then the cayuco scrapes against the sand and stops. The paddle drops from my hands into the water.

I look up.

Many people have gathered. I do not understand the English that they speak, but later I am told that one man shouted very loudly, "It's some of those stinking boat people!"

I hold out my hand. "*Necesitamos ayuda,*" I say in Spanish, trying to tell them that we need help.

"Get out of here!" another man shouts. "This is a private club!"

I do not need to know English to understand the anger in the man's eyes and in the eyes of many others.

But then a tall woman pushes in front of the man. She has a kind look in her eyes. She kicks her shoes off and runs into the water to grab and hold the front of the cayuco. Now others also run into the water to help her. Together they pull the heavy cayuco up onto the sand.

Then hands reach down to help me. I cannot stand, so they must lift me. The tall woman reaches into the cayuco and lifts Angelina in her arms. The plastic doll drops onto the sand. I point, and the woman reaches down and grabs the doll. She carries Angelina and the doll up the beach.

There is much I do not remember because I am so weak, but I remember that people hold my arms. I cannot stand, and so they carry me. A van comes with bright lights that flash. It takes Angelina and me away. I do not know where we go, until they carry us into a bright room and I see nurses and doctors. In Guatemala, we do not go to hospitals because we do not have money. Nurses and doctors are for rich people.

They try to take Angelina away from me into a different room. Angelina screams with a voice that is too loud for a little four-year-old girl. They bring her back, and she holds me tight. A nurse comes to me and she speaks in Spanish. "*Como te llamas?*" she says, asking me my name.

"Santiago," I say. "Santiago Cruz."

"I am Juana," she says, still speaking Spanish. "And what is this little girl's name?"

"This is my sister," I say. "Her name is Angelina. Please do not take her away from me."

"We won't," Juana says. "Where is your home?"

I do not know how to answer this question. "We come from Guatemala," I say.

"And where are your parents?"

"They are dead."

The nurse looks at me with eyes that I do not think believe me. "Then how did you get here?"

"My sister and I, we sailed across the ocean in a cayuco."

27

BLUE SKY

THEY TAKE ANGELINA AND ME into a room that has two tables. "Angelina," I say. "Do not cry now. These people will help us."

"Do not leave me!" she screams. Her cheeks are wet with tears. Fear dances in her eyes.

"I am here," I say. "I will not leave you."

Because she believes me, Angelina stops crying.

Beside me, a nurse works on Angelina. Always Angelina watches to make sure I do not leave. She feels much pain, but the worst suffering is in her eyes. I think this pain will take much longer to heal.

The nurses take off our ragged clothes and they wash our bodies. The nurse that knows Spanish, Juana, talks to me while she is working. "I do not understand your sister when she talks," she says.

"We speak Kekchi," I say. "That is why my Spanish

is not very good. But Angelina understands some Spanish."

"How did you get so many sores?"

"We have been on the ocean for twenty-three days," I say. "Always there was sun and salt water."

Juana tells me they must put needles with tubes into our arms. I think Angelina is going to cry again, but before they put the needle into her arm, I ask Angelina, "Where is your doll?"

Angelina points across the room to a table. When she looks back at me, the needle is already in her arm. The nurse, Juana, smiles at me.

"Will they help my doll?" Angelina asks me.

"Oh, yes," I say. "But first they must help you."

"If you want to help my sister," I tell Juana quietly, "you must also help her doll."

"I think we can do that," Juana says. "And your parents," she asks. "You say they are dead. How did they die?"

This is a very hard question to answer. Now I am the one who cries. "The soldiers," I say. "They came in the middle of the night and burned my village. They killed everyone."

"How did you escape?"

"My mother woke me up and told me the soldiers were coming. She gave me Angelina and told me to run. And so I ran. After I escaped, I looked back and could see the night sky burning red."

Juana gives us water to drink but tells us we cannot eat tonight because maybe they will find broken bones and need to operate. She turns and tells the other nurses something in English. They all look at me and they look at Angelina. The look in their eyes is very kind. Juana asks me many more questions. I try to answer all that I can, but I am very tired. Angelina and I fall asleep before the nurses finish putting bandages on all our sores.

When I wake up, I am lying on a bed in a small room. It is dark, but light comes in through the door, and I can see Angelina beside me in the same bed. I think it is a dream that I am here and not in the cayuco, so I close my eyes and sleep again.

But it is not a dream. When I wake up in the morning, the sun shines through the window like a river of light. Angelina is awake and stares around the room with big eyes. She, too, must think that this is a dream. Both of us have bandages all over our bodies. I have a big bandage on the side of my head where the sail pole has hit me.

"Good morning, Angelina," I say.

She looks at me. Her eyes blink. "Where are we?" she asks.

I smile. "This is the United States of America."

She stares out the window. "I think I like the . . ." She stops. "Where is this again?"

"The United States of America."

She nods. "It is a good place." She looks around the

room. "Did you tip the cayuco over again?"

"Yes, a very big storm made the cayuco tip over."

A nurse hears us talk and comes into the room. It is not Juana, but this nurse also speaks Spanish. "Did you sleep well?" she asks.

I can only nod.

"They tell me that you two sailed the ocean alone," she says.

Again, I nod.

"Did you sail during the storm last night?"

"Yes," I say. "We tipped over."

"That was the worst tropical storm we have had in years."

"I am glad it is over," I say.

"Are you hungry?" she asks.

Angelina nods.

"Yes. Yes, very hungry," I say.

"Well, then, let's get you two something to eat."

The nurse leaves and comes back soon with two trays. "I only want you to eat bread and pudding this morning," she says. "Later today, you can have more."

I do not tell the nurse that bread and pudding will be a feast for us.

"There are some men who want to talk to you after you finish eating, okay?"

"Where is my doll?" asks Angelina.

"The nurses had to work on your doll almost all night because she was hurt so bad," the nurse says. "Juana will bring her to you soon."

"My doll did not die, did she?" Angelina asks.

"No, your doll did not die," says the nurse.

Angelina looks worried, but she does not cry.

We finish eating, and there are two men who come in to visit. They close the door and sit beside our beds in chairs. They speak Spanish, and they say they are from the Immigration and Naturalization Service. I do not know what that is, but I think they are from the government, and this makes me scared, because in my country we are always afraid of the government.

The men are not angry, I do not think. But they do not smile when they ask me questions. When I talk, they write many things on paper. Because they keep asking me about my family, I do not know if they believe me. I do not think they believe that we sailed here. "I will show you the cayuco," I say.

"We have already seen your cayuco," one of the men says. "Where did you learn to sail?"

"I do not know how to sail very much," I say. "My uncle Ramos, he taught me a little, and so did his neighbor, Enrique. Also, the ocean has taught me much. But I do not know all of the names of every part of a boat. I do not know how to read a map or tell you where I am with the stars. No, I am not a sailor."

The man studies me and finally he smiles. "If you sailed from Guatemala in that little canoe, you are one hell of a sailor. And you are either very foolish or very brave."

"I was very scared," I say.

When the men finish, they do not tell me why we have talked or what they are thinking. "We will talk more tomorrow," they say.

When they open the door to leave, there are many more people outside the door. A nurse comes in and tells me the people work for radio and television stations. They want to talk to me about my trip.

I do not care if we talk, but I do not understand why they want to talk to me.

These people also speak to me in Spanish, and again I answer many questions. Angelina is afraid, so she crawls over and sits on my lap. I think everyone likes Angelina, because many times the questions stop and people watch her. They laugh and take pictures of her.

I tell the group the words that Uncle Ramos told me the night he died. "'Go as far away as you can and tell what has happened this night,'" I say. "That is what he told me. I will never forget those words."

And so I tell everything that has happened. Again I cry when I tell about my family dying and about Uncle Ramos and about Carlos with his legs cut off and about the red sky at night. I think I will always cry when I think about those things. I also tell about the white butterflies, the mud in the gas tank, and the pigs in the cayuco. Everyone laughs. I finish by telling about the pirates and the fishhook and the storm. And I tell them about our game, staying alive.

"Tell them about the river of garbage where you found my doll," Angelina tells me.

And so I tell about the river of garbage and about Angelina's broken doll.

"Where is the doll now?" one of the women asks.

Before I can speak, a nurse that is in the room says, "The doll was broken and had a missing arm and was hurt very badly. So we had to work all night to fix her. But I think she is better now." The nurse looks at Angelina. "Do you want to see your doll now?"

Angelina nods very hard.

The nurse Juana walks into the room holding something behind her back. "Close your eyes and hold out your hands," she tells Angelina.

Angelina closes her eyes and puts out her short bandaged arms. I think she is peeking when a brand-new doll is placed in her arms. The doll has long black hair and a new red dress and dark skin as smooth as glass. On the right arm there is a white bandage.

Angelina can only stare. I think there is a light inside her head because her eyes shine so bright. I know she has never seen anything so beautiful. The group claps, and they take many more pictures with their cameras. Angelina hugs the doll. She smiles, and big silent tears fill her eyes. When I see her tears, I think that with time maybe she will be all right.

Before the group leaves, one man tells me we will be on the television tonight. "Is there anything else you wish to say?" he asks.

The group waits for my next words, but I am finished. I shake my head slowly. I can speak no more. Tears have filled my eyes, and the hurt of my memories squeezes my throat like a strong hand.

After the group leaves, later in the afternoon, the nurses change our bandages, and we eat again. This time they let us eat some bread and hot chicken soup. Angelina eats the bread with both hands. I think she will hurt herself if she tries to put any more into her mouth without swallowing. I do not think they will ever bring enough food to fill our stomachs. Later we ask for food again, and we eat. They bring us more soup, tortillas, and tamales.

After the evening meal, Juana turns on the television. I have seen televisions before when I traveled with my father to Lake Izabal. But Angelina has not, and she stares at the moving picture with big silent eyes. Tonight I cannot believe what I see: pictures of the cayuco sitting on a beach and pictures of Angelina and me in the hospital room. I do not understand the English, but Juana tells me everything that is being said. She says that they are telling our story.

Other nurses and a doctor stop in the room to watch what we are seeing. Angelina keeps staring at the television like it is magic. Every time the camera shows her, she claps and screams, "Look at me! Look at me!"

We smile.

After the television is finished showing pictures of us, the doctor and the nurses leave. Juana is busy, so she, too, must leave. But she returns after it is dark and talks with me. We talk very late, long after Angelina falls asleep. I tell Juana about Enrique and Silvia. "Without their help, I do not think we would be alive today," I say. "I wish somehow they could know that we did not die."

Juana is a very nice lady. She reminds me of my mother. I think that I can trust her, so I ask her something very important. "Will your government send Angelina and me back to Guatemala because we do not have our papers?" I ask.

Juana shakes her head and smiles. "After what has happened to you and all the stories about you that ran tonight on the television, you will never have to go back to Guatemala until you want to."

"Someday, I want to go back," I say. "But I do not want to go back until the soldiers stop killing mothers and fathers and children."

"Someday, that time will come," Juana says. "And I think that time will come sooner because of your courage. Until then, the United States will be your new home. It will be hard, because there are many things new and different here. You and Angelina will need to learn English, but you are young and you will learn."

"Thank you for being our friend," I say.

Juana's smile is very kind. Even with Angelina asleep, she says, "Good night, Santiago and Angelina

Cruz. Welcome to America. Now, if I don't get back to work, they'll think I went home." Quietly she turns and leaves.

After she leaves, I lie awake and look up into the black night. For a long time, I am afraid to close my eyes. I wish that Juana was still here talking to me, because I know that when I fall asleep, my dreams will bring back the screams and the guns and the fire. Even now I can see the red skies again. These are things that can never be forgotten.

But finally I do let my eyes close because I am tired. I know that the night will be long—this, I cannot change. But I also know that when the morning comes, the red will disappear and the sun will shine and the sky will be blue again. Maybe someday that is how it will always be. Skies should always be blue.

AUTHOR'S NOTE

MANY ACCOUNTS have documented the tragic military massacres in Central America during the 1980s. In Guatemala alone, more than 450 villages were torched, and tens of thousands of people were tortured and killed. Men were killed first, then women, and lastly the children. Because of this, many children witnessed the atrocities, and some escaped to tell of them. Today a generation of children still carries these memories like scars.

Many Americans dismiss these events simply as tragic. But we, too, share much blame. Our government did, in fact, provide training and weapons to those soldiers who attacked the Guatemalan villages during those nights when the sky glowed red.

Fighting communism was the excuse given by our military leaders to defend these massacres during congressional hearings. But the fact will always remain that most of those killed had never heard of communism and surely were not armed by communists. Most went to their graves armed with only machetes, sticks, and the will to protect their families and homes. This is the will that exists in each of us when all that we know and love is taken away.

My hope is that the mistakes of our past will act as a reminder to our great country that no child, for whatever reason, should ever see a red sky at night.